THE EARTH, THE STARS AND WHISPER

ALSO BY ROBERT REA

A VIEW TO THE NORTH

SUN DREAMS

THE EARTH, THE STARS AND WHISPER

A NOVEL BY

ROBERT REA

MapleLand Press
Ontario, Canada

Cover photograph: Robert Rea

Rea, Robert, 1964-
        The earth, the stars, and whisper

ISBN 0-9686997-3-1

Published by: MapleLand Press
Book design by: Karen Petherick,
                     Intuitive Design International Ltd.,
                     Peterborough, ON
Printed in Canada by: Webcom Limited

NOTICE

ACKNOWLEDGMENTS

The author gratefully acknowledges Marilyn Smart for her advice, ideas, and encouragement throughout the development of this novel.

PART ONE

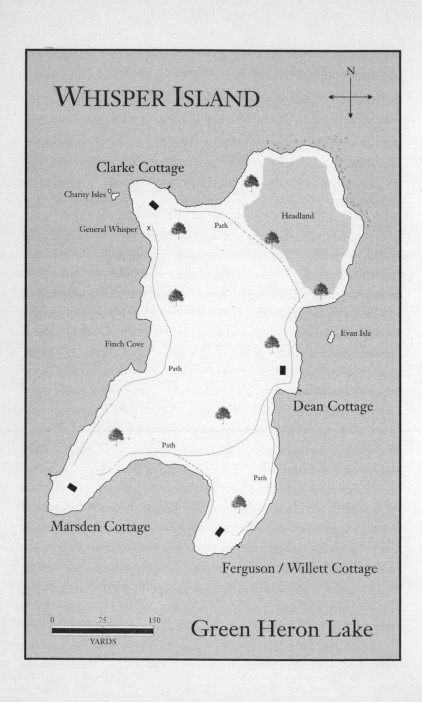

WHISPER ISLAND

N

Clarke Cottage

Charity Isles

General Whisper   x

Path

Headland

Finch Cove

Path

Evan Isle

Dean Cottage

Path

Path

Marsden Cottage

Path

Ferguson / Willett Cottage

0   75   150

YARDS

Green Heron Lake

1

This is a story of both a special community and a special time. Mind, not only the vanquished portrayed herein but also the privileged would hardly admit as much. After the summer of 2002 George Clarke lamented, "The season put us in a doozy of a wiggle, and rarely have a sorry bunch of slobs ever fought so hard to keep a miserable chunk of bush." But then George was never one to get all gooey about himself, others, or the universe in general; he was a "liver, not a lover." For their part his neighbours would remain silently humble through sheer prudence. As you will see, not only failures but successes too are sometimes best kept secret.

Green Heron Lake, a gift left by the glacial gods during their last sojourn south, is nestled deep within Ontario's cottage country. Some twenty unsquare kilometers in area this sprawling body of blue is home to dozens of islands, and one as such is the focus of this tale.

The twentieth century was one quarter fulfilled when Gord and Nora Ferguson first visited Whisper. Honeymooning at a mainland lodge they stopped at the cottageless island, on a whim, for a picnic amid canoe touring. Green Heron residents would later speak of their chosen rest stop as merely that; none held it in high regard. But between this and future visits the Fergusons became smitten by this curious collage of pink and silvery granite, reddish earth, and thick green forest. So smitten that when the island came up for sale in 1933 they parted with nearly all worldly possessions to buy it. A boat and modest cabin followed, and thereafter Whisper became, if in their eyes only, a cherished summer retreat. "We've found our own little Eden," a sparkle-eyed Nora Ferguson proclaimed with chin and glass held high. And so it seemed.

Some forty summer seasons would pass before the Fergusons discovered they were not alone. When failing health rendered them unfit for regular travel north they saw no choice but to say goodbye to Whisper. It was then the aging couple realized others, through their own unplanned rest stops, had also come to appreciate their brand of paradise.

George Clarke arrived on the scene first, buying one of four newly established island lots in autumn of 1973. The Marsdens and Deans followed suit a year later, and lastly, in 1975, Marcy Willett made Whisper her summer refuge. An island community thus formed, and until their last days the Fergusons referred to these descendants as their "cottage kids."

Sadly, those last days for both Gord and Nora would soon arrive. On a sunny August afternoon in 1977 the "kids" held a quiet memorial on Whisper's northern headland, and an ever present breeze spread ashes over a desired final resting place. But as those original residents also wished, cottaging tradition continued on this generally disparaged island. Indeed, twenty-five years later the same community — surprisingly, to most — remained intact.

Tom and Dorothy Burke were among those who found Whisper a veritable conversation piece. The middle-aged couple had a cottage on the mainland to the west of the island. Over the years they'd become good friends with all of Whisper's cottagers, and during visits had both heard and observed much. And although not particularly nosy, they couldn't help occasionally reflecting on the rugged island that was distant yet clearly viewed from their front deck.

One such conversation took place late on a Friday evening in May of 2002, just after the couple returned from playing cards with Pam and Roger Marsden.

As Tom bare-footed across a moonlit deck to their chairs with several nightcaps, Dorothy asked, "So you really don't think they even gave it much thought?"

Handing over a "Green Heron Gooser" the bartender seated himself with his own and answered, "Didn't sound like it. And I felt the place would have been perfect for them — good location on the lake, shipshape cottage, and a nice smooth, level lot for Pammy's poor hip joints."

"She'd probably have better luck with her early morning jogging, or whatever that was we saw years back."

"True. They'd both also be away from what's forever waiting to happen next door."

Dorothy grimaced. "Now, now. He's faring much better these days, I think."

Returning a mischievous grin, Tom countered with, "Oh, I suppose, and I do love the guy, but Evan's well ... *still Evan*. As Sir John Dean himself once said, 'I cannot forecast to you the action of my son. He is a misfortune wrapped in an accident inside a disaster.'

"You're both very cruel. But that said, the Marsdens are staying put on Whisper?"

"Staying put. And as we've talked about a hundred times, I don't have a clue why. For that matter I don't know why any of them have stayed for so long. Ol' George Clarke strikes me as a bull in a china shop over there, Evan has some unfortunate history he'd surely like to forget, and I fear poor Marcy will one day either try walking or dancing her way to the 'mother ship', Lord help her."

"Her sweetie would save her."

"Yes, maybe George would, my clever precious, but you get the idea." Tom now lovingly sipped his drink and continued with, "To me the biggest mystery of all, though, is why anyone else in their right mind would want so badly that rocky, bush-snarled excuse for an island, assuming that's what they're after."

"Did Roger update you on police progress. Are they getting anywhere?"

"No, and I'm not overly surprised. They've yet to find any fingerprints, and obviously it'd be pretty tough keeping watch over a small island in the middle of a decent-sized lake."

Dorothy, who'd been gazing all this time at distant lights on Whisper, emitted a lengthy sigh. "Well, regardless of how little I care for the island, or how puzzling I find their sticking together, I still feel sorry for that crew. Pam joked enough about the vandalism when we were playing cards, but when I was alone with her later she got downright teary-eyed. She said their little community was 'bigger than most saw, and likewise more close-knit,' whatever that means. She also said to them it seemed indestructible, and that they'd all cottage there, like the Fergusons basically did, to their dying day."

Also now gazing toward the lights of Whisper, Tom added, "Yes. Or so they thought."

2

George Clarke woke very early the middle Saturday of June, 2002. His night table clock showed only 5:32 a.m, but he wasn't surprised. At Whisper he'd unfortunately grown accustomed to early morning risings, and typically to several during the night; the slightest noise outside had become seemingly enough to rouse and draw him to the windows. More than once he'd even slipped out and silently crept about his pitch-black lot, hoping to catch "his buddies" in the act, consequences be damned. Cottage life had been this way two years now.

As had also become routine, soon after rising George padded to his large front window to scan his yard. Once upon a time, he sadly reflected, he made this trip to gauge the weather and consider pleasant plans for the day. But that was once upon.

At this hour the sun had barely risen above the trees on the far eastern mainland. The lake and front yard on this northwestern side of the island thus remained much bathed in mist and shadow. Visibility was still sufficient, however, to reveal something absent from its traditional home, and soon after, that same something decidedly elsewhere.

Forming a broad right fist, George roared, "What in the bloody hell *now*?!"

After merely pulling on work pants and boots he shot out the front door, quickly descended the deck stairs, and charged east along the island's boulder-riddled northern shore. Luckily the flag pole of his treasured wooden boat — *The Pride of Whisper* — had become snagged among the shore's overhanging tree branches, and in a spot free of boulders. When he reached the craft he found it had not, however, escaped its cruise unscathed: its port side bore two long and nasty scratches. "Damn it all!" George snarled, and immediately he began removing his boots.

With his pants soon temporarily draped over a shoulder, he waded out. Expending considerable effort from waist-high water, he managed to hoist his big, sixty-seven-year-old frame into the boat. Using a paddle he then coaxed the soon unsnagged boat into deeper water and, to his amazement, succeeded in starting it. Within another minute his cherished craft was therefore home and again tied to its dock.

In addition to studying further the hull scratches, George inspected the heavy chain he'd used to presumably prevent the boat from parting his company. Very clearly it had been cut with a hacksaw, and he speculated on the level of noise such a chore produced. Whoever was responsible was clearly both bold and determined; although the light rain during the night would have masked some of the noise, he nonetheless felt it a miracle he wasn't woken.

Perceiving no security option available other than replacing the single chain with several, George soon headed for his shed. The small building sat nestled among white birches some twenty yards southeast of the dock and was reached by a well-trodden path. With the night's rain it was presently also a muddy path, and as chance had it, this circumstance rendered a second discovery this morning.

The islanders had long assumed several teenage boys were responsible for what now totalled a dozen acts of vandalism on Whisper. The wiry Dempster brothers, both in their early teens, were infamous on Green Heron for being hell-raisers. And in June of the previous summer they'd suffered a harsh encounter with George and neighbour Roger Marsden. Nabbed outside the lake's general store pegging Roger's car with stones — their brand of amusement — the boys soon received hefty punishments from contacted parents. Thereafter, or so went the theory, the two began exacting revenge.

Thus far, however, police had yet to discover anything directly linking the boys to Whisper's vandalism. That all such acts had occurred on weekends — the only time the boys were present on the lake — the islanders recognized as positive but obviously insufficient evidence. Accordingly, frustrations were rising.

Concerning his own misfortunes, George Clarke had long been puzzled by a particular circumstance. His lot had by far the most soil cover of any on Whisper — the others much rockier — yet no search following vandalism yielded tracks. The boys were either careful to not make footprints or equally careful to destroy those they did.

But, during their latest 'mission', they seemingly slipped up at last.

In a patch of mud next to his shed path George spotted several quite distinct boot prints. His immediate reaction was to continue onward, and what he discovered did not surprise him: his shed door was broken and his hacksaw was missing from the workbench's pegboard. That recognized, he soon returned to the prints and studied them closer. It was then he noticed something that indeed surprised him.

Although George Clarke was a large man and walked the

earth brandishing size twelves, the prints before him were decidedly longer and wider. "Bloomin' flippers," Pam Marsden would later declare. By their depth George also judged they belonged to a fellow of similar weight to him, meaning over two hundred pounds. And further contradicting a certain theory, despite a lengthy search George discovered no prints indicating a companion.

Whatever man had borrowed his hacksaw the previous night, he was apparently working alone.

About three hours later, ensconced in his official chair in what once was the Fergusons' kitchen and what now was Marcy Willett's, George shared his morning's discoveries with his fellow islanders. Pam and Roger Marsden sat opposite him while young Evan Dean helped Marcy make breakfast — on this morning a small mountain of pancakes. Following a long established tradition, the cottagers assembled as such every Saturday on Whisper, taking turns as host.

Smoothing ruffled black hair, and anxiously drumming the table with slender, freckled fingers, Roger Marsden said to George, "I still contend, though, Ken Sheppard could easily have made the tracks last weekend. He's a tall guy who might well have big feet on him, and when we visited your shed he could have stepped where you mentioned."

"And I can't call to confirm all that?"

Roger shook his head. "Last Monday he headed west somewhere for the summer to see family. That's why he needed your chain saw in a hurry last Sunday; he wanted to fell a dead tree beside his cottage before leaving. But anyway — since we can't check on Ken — for now yours truly is sticking with the Dempster boys. Besides, have you honestly thought of anybody else yet that might have this strong a grudge against us?"

George shrugged.

"Me neither. The boys, though, I can definitely see vandalizing us. They also strike me as just clever enough not to leave fingerprints, and to spot and smash that security camera I set up."

Pam, who'd been browsing a medical journal, now said to George, "I don't know if Roger told you, but he had another talk with their father."

George's eyes lit up. "Really! And what excuses did you get this time?"

Roger grinned. "None, believe it or not. Frank seemed pretty open this round to admitting his boys might — 'as long shots' — be the culprits. I don't know if he'll ever deny his long shots a trip to the lake until they're actually caught, but I'm hoping he'll at least treat them to a chat. That might just worry them enough to quit."

"Yeah. And go terrorizing someone else," Pam quipped, now rising awkwardly from her chair and stretching. "This ailing bod's had about enough."

George countered with, "Sure, Pammy, but then I'd miss the intense pleasure of catching them, wouldn't I?" Rubbing a large, well-worn fist inside another paw, he added, "After the whole *Pride* affair this morning, I've been dreaming of that night."

Pam smiled. "How is your baby, anyway? Do the new scratches match well with the forty-seven others?"

George's back rose. "You watch your tongue, young lady. That's boat's a classic."

Considering past occasions, George would have continued his rant had it not been for a huge plate of pancakes, which now arrived in fine style courtesy of Evan Dean. A moment later both he and Marcy joined the others at the table and the 'festivities' began.

Staring at his loaded plate, while his neighbours dug in, Roger said to Evan, "Now ... Marcy made these, right? You just carried them to the table?"

After delivering a swat, Pam said, "Don't take it from him, Ev."

"Yes," piped in Marcy, waving an index finger for added effect. "Your hair looks wonderful today." To Pam she said, "Don't you just love his sandy blonde? I really must find a wig that colour."

Not side-tracked, Evan defensively spouted in all directions, "Okay, so Marcy made them, but I'm getting better with cooking. I really am."

Grinning, Roger said, "So next time you host we'll only be ill a week?"

Ignoring this, Evan continued proudly with, "I'm doing everything right these days. I haven't messed up with anything in ages. Right, George? Tell'em."

After finalizing a generous mouthful, George said, "A fine, upstanding lad this Evan's become. Twenty-four goin' on the big eighty-four in the wisdom department. Yesiree. Can't say enough."

Roger smiled. "So you need to borrow his wheelbarrow again, then?"

Innocently turning to Evan, George said, "Is it free this morning?"

Amid laughter, Marcy's phone rang and she politely excused herself. She would normally leave the phone during a meal but all knew she was expecting an important call.

Once she was out of hearing range George, now calm again, paused from his breakfast and caught Pam's eye. A short gaze followed by one directed at his pancakes proved sufficient.

In a whisper came, "Not up to her usual standards?"

George nodded, then looked quizzically toward the living room, where Marcy was now engaged in a typically animated conversation, one arm flailing about while she talked a mile a minute.

"We were short on a lot of things today," said Evan, tenderly. "I let it go because I thought Marcy'd be hurt if I went to my place for stuff. Guess she slipped up on her groceries this weekend."

"No," Pam again whispered, glancing at Evan before training her eyes on George. "I wish it were only that. I'm afraid the problem is a touch more serious."

George stared back at her. "You mean she's *hurting*? How the heck can she be hurting? Oliver left her a trunk full, God rest his soul."

Pam shrugged. "Don't know how. But I'm convinced she is. I can tell you she's been late a few times in Toronto giving us rent for the basement apartment. Take her birthday present, too. Marcy ogled that thing twenty seven times in Birchport last summer and still didn't buy it."

In celebration of Marcy's sixty-eighth birthday several weeks earlier, the islanders pooled their funds and presented her with a very special gift. It was one, as Roger slyly put it, "unlike any other": a life-size, papier mâché fawn coated with birch chips, and sporting twigs for antlers (an unusually mature fawn), chunks of fungi for ears, and a spruce branch for a tail. For three years, shockingly, this two-hundred-dollar-and-falling item had sat in 'The Birchport Gallery' short a buyer. To Marcy, though, it had long been "simply the most adorable thing ever made." Transferring it to the island the day prior to Marcy's birthday, Pam somehow couldn't stop tittering.

That said, when Marcy returned to the kitchen table from her phone call Pam delivered, "We were just talking about your nifty birthday present. Where did it go, anyway? I didn't see it in your room."

Marcy answered, "He's all cozy in the porch right now. But I'd like him in my bedroom, in front of my window. I need George to move my cedar chest, though."

Pam smiled. "Oh, I'm sure your sweetie will look after it. Won't you, sweetie?"

"Bugger off."

After a failed attempt at kissing George's cheek, Pam again turned to Marcy. "Anyway — sorry if I'm being nosy — but did Linda have much to report?"

"Yes! All is shaping up beautifully. We now have a little group of musicians organized to play for us. So our scouting mission for them, and the one for our napkins, was well worth my missing last weekend here."

George blinked hard. "For your blessed *nap*—?"

Truncating this remark, Pam said, "Wonderful! Sounds like you're in for the family reunion of the century. Good for you — I'm so happy for you."

As Marcy glowed her way to the kitchen sink with empty plates, Roger said, "So when is the big day again?"

"Second last weekend of the summer," said Pam.

"Saturday the twenty-fourth of August," Marcy echoed more officially.

"We can only hope it goes over with a bang," George offered, winking at a smiling Evan.

Decidedly less jokingly, Roger stared at George and quietly said, "All considering, Mr. Clarke, we should probably hope it doesn't."

Soon after breakfast the islanders dispersed, leaving only George at Marcy's. He stayed to continue with a project started the previous weekend. The two paths leading from Marcy's place — those enabling, foremost, the security offered by her neighbours — were "clearly hurting." This he'd declared during the Saturday breakfast at Pam and Roger's, and with the grinning hosts only nodding, he shared a critical plan to fetch gravel from his mainland stockpile.

He progressed only as far as delivering the gravel to shore near Marcy's dock that previous weekend, so there remained the chore of moving it by wheelbarrow to the paths. In executing this transfer George expected a long day; like all the lots on Whisper, Marcy's was a tangle of trees, thick shrubs, and tortured bedrock.

As it went, though, the work proved not too taxing. He managed to find a relatively easy route between shore and paths, and was left puzzled why such jobs had proven so tedious in past. Initially he considered he was simply feeling a touch more spry than usual. Then, however, he made yet another discovery this day. During one of his return trips to the dock, he suddenly stopped and put down Evan's wheelbarrow.

In the direction of the cottage he hollered, "*Marcy?*"

The cottage's owner soon appeared and cheerfully answered from her front deck. "Yes, dear?"

With a painfully wrinkled forehead, George said, "Correct me if I'm wrong, but ... did I not build a big stone planter here a few years back?" He pointed at the ground to his right.

"Why, yes you did, George."

"And ... where might I ask is that planter now?"

"I don't know for sure. I noticed it missing when the Marsdens delivered me here yesterday. Gladys Lockhart said it was delightful when she visited for tea last year, though. Do you think maybe she borrowed it for the summer, George? If she did she's quite welcome to. I really wouldn't worry."

With that, and a quick reminder of a lovely lunch approaching, Marcy returned inside.

"Maybe she bor—?!" George closed his eyes and vigorously scratched his head.

He studied the ground where the four by eight foot stone planter had stood. Whoever was responsible for the deed had done a clean job — not only was there no sign of the several hundred river stones he'd used, but also no sign of the soil. In fact, you could barely even see the imprint of where the planter had stood. No wonder he hadn't immediately noticed this former obstruction missing.

His question now was: where did all the rocks and soil go?

Naturally he first searched Marcy's waterfront. Since the vandal had evidently done his work the previous weekend, the soil could well have dispersed by now, but obviously not the river stones. Even, however, with the bright morning offering a clear view of the lake bottom to some twenty feet out from shore, he saw no sign of the stones.

Next he scoured Marcy's yard — to no avail — followed by the woods immediately behind her cottage. He seriously questioned someone hauling the stones that far, but he checked anyway. Once again, though, not even a hint.

It was while returning from the woods Marcy yelled to him lunch was ready, and feeling obliged, he defeatedly stepped inside. Once back in his chair he mostly stewed the next half hour. He'd devoted several weekends years earlier to building that stone planter for Marcy, and she had loved it, literally doing a little dance around it when it was finished and full of flowers. Yes, he could build her a new one, but what was the point? So someone could have another laugh at their expense?

In such a glum mood did George soon rise to resume his path repairs. Just before he stepped out, however, Marcy reminded him about moving her bedroom's cedar chest. This, of course, to make space for her cherished "birthday deer."

Now while leading the way to her room, Marcy happened to mention, "Must be my years adding up, but I used to be able to move the chest myself."

If this remark only pushed George halfway to his awakening, his subsequent inability to budge the cedar chest even an inch easily finished the job.

Opening the lid, he already knew.

Not only was the cedar chest filled with dirty, cement-crusted stones, George soon found another load piled in Marcy's closet, and yet more under her bed.

As he stood stock still with mouth agape, surveying all, Marcy said, "Goodness! Why would there be stones in my room? Dear?"

In response George could only eventually manage, softly, "I really don't know, Marcy. Please don't fuss over it, though. I'm sure it's just someone playing ... a little joke."

And before his explosion of anger, which would come later and in private, George turned and headed for the door. This time a yard search, one with a different focus, yielded results.

Close to Marcy's side door, and evidently only imprinted in packed earth through their owner hauling heavy loads, were huge and familiar boot prints.

Stunned beyond measure, George said merely to himself, "What in *heaven's name* is happening around here?!"

3

"Did you do it?" Glenna Clarke asked with a hushed voice, beaming a crazed smile. "Did you give 'er a nice hefty swing for your dear mother, big George? Did you now?"

"I did."

Thus triggered, Glenna hopped about the living room in filthy bare feet and slapped at her torn slacks, in so doing spilling some of her drink. "Haaaa! Then I can't bloody *wait* to see the old coot's face when he comes home. This is just *too* juicy!"

As his mother went to their cracked front window and peeked behind a closed and tattered curtain, George headed for what passed as their hall closet. Soon he said, "Have you seen my work boots, ma?"

When he received no answer he returned to the living room. His mother's face was still buried behind the curtain, and he heard her talking to herself.

"I said — have you seen my work boots?"

Glenna pulled away from the window and stared vacantly at George a moment, seemingly clueless to what he was asking. At last she pulled her cigarette from her mouth, and through exhaled smoke said, "Maybe your brother has them. How the hell would I know?" A scarred and prematurely-aged face then brightened again. "Besides, who cares about stupid *boots*? The show's soon to begin, baby. Come! Come and sit by the window with me."

"I've got stuff to do, ma."

"Your work's done for the day, Georgie! And what fine work it was. Com'on, big boy — come and have a drink with me."

"Maybe later. I've got stuff to do."

As George walked off to his ramshackle bedroom, his mother raced from the window and yelled down the hall, "I'll let you know when the fun begins, Georgie. You'll come have a drinkie-pooh with your mother *then*, won't you?"

"Sure."

George Clarke was only about nine when he began wondering why he or his older brother Ian were brought into the world. He'd already become wise enough to the ways of that world to realize his mother and father were not exactly ideal parents. Cal Clarke had met Glenna Vair at a Manitoba tavern he frequented during his truck runs from Toronto to Calgary. Glenna did more than wait on tables, and as she later told her sons, both were products of what she jokingly called "moonlighting."

Whether he was truly responsible for the two boys Glenna eventually brought forth Cal Clarke probably never knew. But Glenna's arguments (or persuasive skills) were apparently sufficient, because within several years of George's birth the 'family' had a home in western Ontario. Cal provided for Glenna a bargain-basement farmhouse at the end of a long gravel side road, in a tiny, six-house community known as Blackwell.

As though George and brother Ian needed a rougher hand in life, Blackwell proved extremely cold and unwelcoming. The very day Cal and Glenna moved in with the boys, in fact, a shirtless, beer-bellied man in his forties strolled over to point out the location of property stakes. That set the tone for neighbourly relations to come.

Over roughly the next fifteen years Cal and Glenna would unsurprisingly engage in countless domestic disputes, but clashes with fellow community members ultimately took front stage. No one, apparently, got along with anyone else in Blackwell. Why each resident remained clearly became a matter of, "they're not driving *me* out." This tiny village was therefore perpetually in a state of war, and over the years battles became increasingly intense.

Cal's first major run-in was with a next-door neighbour named Bill Adamson, the property stake notifier. When Bill decided he'd try out a new stereo he'd picked up (stolen) at 2:00 a.m. one night, a fight between him and Cal broke out in the Adamsons' yard. By the time police handcuffed the two battered men and carted them off, six of the Adamsons' windows were smashed. Naturally Bill soon returned the favour, and Cal, sitting near one of his own windows, wound up requiring over a hundred stitches to his face. This, of course, sent him off on an "errand." And so on.

Countless cyclical battles such as this occurred in Blackwell, many involving the Clarkes. To young George it seemed his father no sooner returned home from a long road run than he was battling with a neighbour. Glenna had a hand in this; while Cal was away she stirred up all manner of trouble, getting George and Ian — both large boys — to do the dirty work for her. So the very minute Cal returned home he was up against trouble. Such went on for years, and where it eventually led struck childhood-denied George as entirely predictable.

Blackwell's most serious incident occurred in the spring of 1953, the year George turned eighteen. Late one evening, after fighting at length with a now alcoholic Glenna, Cal Clarke left the family for good. But just before he made his exit he was gracious enough to drive his rig into the house of Dunc Silvey, a neighbour Cal least enjoyed. George didn't know whether his father intended to, but in the process he put Dunc's visiting aunt in the hospital. Worse, two weeks later she passed away.

Revenge, of course, was inevitable. George woke one morning to soon realize his brother had not come home the previous night. Neither he nor Glenna worried too much that day, but on the second George began searching for Ian. His first stop was Dunc Silvey's place, but naturally he "knew nothing" and promptly slammed the door. Just before doing so, however, he offered a very evil smirk, and that was all George needed to realize he wouldn't be seeing his brother again.

The police never found Ian's body, and thus no charges were ever laid. Glenna reacted to the loss of her eldest son with a drunken mix of mourning and unawareness Ian was even absent — frequently she still mentioned him as though he were in the house. As for George, several weeks after his brother disappeared he reacted another way.

He wasn't long in packing his meagre possessions that Tuesday evening his mother sent him to smash a neighbour's windshield with a sledge hammer. Why this neighbour was the chosen victim of the day he didn't know and didn't care.

"I'm goin' away for a few days, ma," he said at the front door.

Apparently not truly hearing him, Glenna, back at the window, said, "Be home by five, though. Johnny Windshield over there will probably want a word with you." She then emitted a guttural laugh that quickly degenerated into a bout of smoker's hack.

They were the last sounds George ever heard from his mother. He soon drove his truck past his neighbour's pickup — one with its windshield still entirely intact — and headed for the highway.

If George gained anything from living in the fine community of Blackwell, it was a few carpentry skills. This, ironically, from helping his father repair their house after 'visits' by neighbours. With this experience now to his credit, George soon found work with a busy building contractor in Whitby. A small house followed within a few years, and for roughly the next several decades George's life actually became fairly peaceful and normal. This, at least, he would have contended.

The fact was, fellow employees at Dawson Construction considered George anything but normal. He had a serious reputation for being hard-nosed and unsociable. So unpopular did he become, in fact, that Vince Dawson almost had to let him go. As it went, the employer reserved George for work he could do alone, a "cleanup man" who looked after small jobs or who applied finishing touches to larger projects. Vince thus kept his ranks satisfied and also retained in George a pretty decent carpenter.

One small job popped up in early May of 1972. A regular city client of Vince's, Gord Ferguson wanted work done to his cottage. The job would entail staying at the Fergusons' place several weeks. Vince figured George fit the bill, and thought he'd welcome the escape from the city.

He was wrong, but with work scarce this month George

nonetheless took the job, leaving for Green Heron the following Monday. The drive, as he feared, was not pleasant; every negative memory of growing up in rural Ontario seemed to return in those several hours. On two occasions he even stopped his truck and almost abandoned the whole mission.

But continuing, George reached Green Heron about 11:00 a.m. He soon found the Fergusons left a tin boat for him at what they called "Ferg Landing." This consisted of a tiny mainland lot the couple owned that served as a mini-marina for the island.

Loaded up and slowly cruising across the lake about a half hour later, George's first impression of Whisper Island was similar to that of most. The boulder-riddled, tree-snarled body of land struck him as the last place anyone would want a cottage. It also puzzled him that its sole inhabitants were spending money on the repairs he was about the make. Vince Dawson informed him the Fergusons planned to sell soon, and George couldn't see the couple getting their repair expenses back in the sale. They could, he figured, build the Taj Mahal on this island and still get next to nothing for it.

The Fergusons' cottage indeed proved in rough shape. It badly needed levelling, the roof and plumbing were leaking, and many of the deck planks broke under George's weight. Myriad other problems also needed tending to, and the carpenter wound up making a list. In the end he figured three weeks might be required, and consequently he was even more convinced the job was a foolish expense. Surely the place wasn't worth all this. But, adopting the standard tradesman's 'paid by the hour' attitude, George set about his labours shortly after unloading the boat and settling into the cottage.

Work progressed well his first week, and thus pleased,

George granted himself a trip each evening to the nearby village of Birchport. Here he would typically grab a few groceries and then sit in a tavern, sipping a beer and generally avoiding anyone who attempted conversation. When returning to the island he would head straight for bed.

On the weekend, however — deciding the tavern would be too busy for his liking — George decided to try a little fishing. This he had not done since leaving Blackwell almost twenty years earlier. Borrowing a rod and some tackle from the Fergusons' shed, he naturally found himself a touch rusty. Nonetheless, for several hours on the nights of Friday, Saturday, and Sunday, he stood on the Fergusons' dock casting.

That habit continued the following week. In addition, George found himself rising early to stroll about Whisper. Despite still considering the island rather ugly, he enjoyed the fresh, clean air in his lungs and the earthy smells of the lake and woods. These were things that again took him back to his childhood, but now in a positive way. Also, it seemed to him, in a justified way. "Shouldn't be holding the bush responsible for people problems," he told himself several times. And such thoughts lingered.

At the end of George's second week, and close to the end of his work, Gord and Nora Ferguson arrived as scheduled to spend the weekend. George initially thought their visit was purely to check his workmanship, and was therefore defensive. Soon enough, however, a short conversation with Gord dispelled that thinking.

"So have you had any fun amongst the work?" he asked as he approached George. This the frail, sparsely gray-haired man did slowly, his health clearly having seen better days.

"A little here and there, I guess," George politely answered. "I've caught a few fish."

"Take a tour, though?"

"Couple of times."

"And what did you conclude?"

"She's ... pleasant enough."

Gord smiled. "Most folk on the lake don't think much of this big rock. They figure the lake'd be better off if the whole island sunk, if that were possible."

"So you're wanting to increase the appeal of the place before you sell?" George asked, tenderly, motioning to the little gazebo he was repairing.

Gord shook his head. "Your work has nothing to do with that; it's just about our own enjoyment." Somberly, Gord added, "Both Nora and I are hurting these days, I'm afraid, and almost for sure this is our last summer coming to Whisper. This is our final 'hurrah,' and we wanted the cottage shipshape for it. We owe it that much, too."

Somewhat dishonestly, George said, "Never know, mister — you might be coming here for years yet."

Gord again smiled. "Nice of you to say, but ... we're realists. We may not be leaving this world for a while after this summer, but travelling up here will soon be beyond us."

"So when did you plan to sell?"

"We'll be listing in the fall. We're breaking the island up into four lots, and selling the empty three, with all proceeds to our charities. Our son's getting the lot with the cottage, and we're signing over that inheritance right away. We figure — why make him wait?"

"All sounds pretty considerate, and especially the charity idea."

"Thank ya."

George now eyed Gord. "I'm curious about something, though."

"What's that?"

"You said most folk on the lake don't care for the island. So ... what drew you and Nora to it?"

Gord mulled a moment, then answered, "The country air, the privacy, and maybe a little magic."

"The magic?"

"Whisper's a place that can get into your bones, somehow. I know it got into Nora's and mine forty or so years ago, and it's still in them today." Gord paused, then said, "You ever have a place sort of *get you* like that?"

George was quick to answer, "'Fraid so, but not in a good way."

"Sorry to hear."

"So am I."

Gord now concluded with, "Well, I hope you do find a place one day — a guy can use that in his life. And if you're ever interested in one of these lots, son, give us a call."

Not even considering this a possibility, George nonetheless politely answered, "Keep that in mind."

For reasons he couldn't quite put his finger on, George wound up making a call to Gord the following spring. Within several weeks he was the owner of Whisper's northwestern lot, and over the summer and autumn he spent most weekends building a modest cabin. This he achieved mostly with materials provided by a generous city boss. Every Friday George would load his pickup with all manner of new and used lumber scraps from job sites, and in time also loaded a cargo trailer he acquired. The resulting cabin looked somewhat tacky and amateurish, but he felt savings on materials more than compensated. He also wasn't overly concerned with appearances.

Despite all this work, George still managed some recreation. About twenty yards off his shoreline were two tiny islets — named 'Charity Isles' by the Fergusons — and around them George found good luck with fishing. He also came to enjoy cruising the lake; this in a wooden runabout the Fergusons included with the lot, an aged but sturdy craft they dubbed *The Pride of Whisper*. Lastly, during winter months he began exploring Green Heron and its surrounding woods by snowmobile, picking up a used "gem" at a Birchport auction. Through numerous outings he came to know the region well and in so doing found great enjoyment. Nestled in front of a crackling woodstove following a trail run, he usually had his head buried in a map planning his next trip.

During his first year George had the island entirely to himself. Since listing the available lots the Fergusons' health had further declined, and they proved correct in guessing the summer of 1972 would be their last at Whisper. Their son Reed, curiously, also no longer visited the family cottage. But George knew he'd eventually be 'blessed' with neighbours, and often while contemplating this inevitability he was haunted by memories of life in Blackwell. Through this experience he ultimately decided the future owners of Whisper's other lots, regardless of their nature, would be keeping to themselves. The countryside he may have allowed back into his life, but of neighbours he'd seen his fill for this lifetime, thanks.

Some of those other owners came on the scene in the spring of 1974. First Pam and Roger Marsden, then John and Emily Dean, began building cottages, the Marsdens on Whisper's southwestern point and the Deans midway along the island's eastern shore. With both couples hiring contractors but nonetheless doing considerable work themselves, over the summer of 1974 George largely received his wish of complete privacy. At no time did any neighbour offer him more than a wave from a distance, and if any happened to encounter him at Ferg Landing conversation was gloriously minimal.

It was in autumn of that year George's luck changed. Amid adding more spikes to his deck planks he caught sight of Pam and Roger Marsden approaching along shore. Both were apparently in their late twenties and bore smiles, and from experience George considered this an ominous sign. In Blackwell younger neighbours especially used smiles as camouflage. This to get in your house or at least close enough to throw something at it.

Since first laying eyes on Pam Marsden George could clearly see she was physically challenged. She walked both stiffly and awkwardly, and there seemed almost a twist to her body, her lower half not quite lining up somehow with her upper. Whatever physical limitations she might have endured, however, she did not strike George as a 'frail, meek little thing.' Sporting rather flamboyant curly brown hair, her piercing blue eyes and bold demeanour spoke of a person not at all lacking in back bone or confidence.

Her husband struck George as equally dangerous. Although possessing a thin, bony frame, scruffy black hair, and an almost sickly white complexion, Roger Marsden nonetheless also seemed the captain of his own ship. To George he appeared a moody sort, too — a fellow whose fuse length varied with the day and perhaps, so to speak, with what he'd had for breakfast. In short, he was the type you were afraid to turn your back on, smiles and jokes be damned.

In light of such assessments, when the Marsdens reached his place George immediately said in a firm voice, "What can I do for you?"

Not at all taken aback, Pam Marsden replied with, "The real question is — what *can't* a brawny, handy fellow like you do for us?"

"What's that sup—?"

"I'm Pam Marsden, and this guy who worships the ground upon which I tread is Roger. We've come to meet our neighbour."

"Well ... sorry but I'm kind of bus—"

"Whether he wants to be met, or not."

Pam and George now went eye to eye. Believe it or not, though, it was the six-foot-two, two hundred and forty pound 'brawny, handy' one of the pair who first looked away.

So it was that George soon had Pam and Roger in for coffee and a half hour chat. And while George did little of the talking — only speaking, really, when asked a question — he nonetheless survived the experience. If his neighbours had ulterior motives for their visit, he never caught them. In fact, when the Marsdens left they even offered the loan of anything they had that their neighbour didn't. Strange talk indeed.

George met John and Emily Dean, toting their year-old son, Evan, about two weeks later. He had just arrived at the landing when the Deans came into the dock in their small aluminum boat. Once again George had little choice but to share a few words with these neighbours, and once again he parted their midst puzzled. *Seemingly* they were harmless.

In the year that followed George would continue warming, slowly but surely, to his fellow islanders. Eventually he allowed John and Roger to join him on his fishing outings, and they even provided him with a few laughs. One evening in August of 1975, for instance, Roger managed to fall out of the boat 'hauling in' what proved a two-pound bass. On another evening, however, that same neighbour showed himself quite co-ordinated. During a thunderstorm a huge pine on George's lot — one the Fergusons nicknamed 'General Whisper' — was struck by lightning. George scrambled to put out a small fire about ten feet up the tree, only to be replaced by a very proficient Roger Marsden. He'd heard the strike and immediately come running. As for Pam Marsden, George "got sucked into" a game of dominoes one afternoon, got soundly defeated, and thereafter resolved to regain his pride. The two played a dozen times the summer of 1975.

The 'capper' event in George's integration into Whisper's community was the arrival of Marcy Willett in autumn of 1975. A widowed niece of Gord and Nora Ferguson, she purchased Whisper's original cottage from Reed Ferguson, Gord and Nora's son and Marcy's cousin. From Marcy her fellow islanders never learned the details of the sale, but apparently she bought the cottage sight unseen. At no time had they witnessed her looking at the property beforehand, and she maintained she had never once visited the Fergusons.

That absorbed, the islanders were not curious long about this peculiar arrangement. Indeed, within several minutes of meeting Marcy, Pam was "entirely clear on the issue."

"I see you're quite a gardener," she said with a bright smile to the island's newest resident, who was tending to planter boxes on her front deck.

"Why thank you!" Marcy returned. "Aren't these orange marigolds just delightful!? I must say they're my favourite. Although, I don't like to play favourites. Especially with cutlery and what have you."

"Uh ... *yes*," said Pam. "I'm ... much the same with cutlery. Now, do you enjoy indoor plants as well?"

"Heavens no! I'm a fresh air gardener, and I like my flowers to be fresh air flowers too. Oh no! Those little windowsill cactuses are not for me. Nor blue curtains. I find they blend with the sky too much. My goodness — you can't even tell if the silly things are open or not!"

With that, Marcy resumed transplanting her marigolds.

All told, on this day Pam might have perceived Marcy as an avid gardener whose mind simply 'wandered a touch' while intensely engaged in her passion. She would have, that is, if it hadn't been early November, and a light snow wasn't falling.

Dear Marcy. Here fellow islanders would find endless puzzlement, and in a kindly, sympathetic sort of way — amusement. She was "a riddle never to be solved," as Pam put it; a veritable smorgasbord of 'new ideas' about the world, 'uniquely wonderful' mannerisms, and 'special' habits. That specialness was perhaps no more evident than in her dress, and, specifically, her hair style. All but bald, Marcy always wore a wig, and within the span of a month, seemingly always a different one. "Which Marcy is with us today?" became a long-running joke among the islanders, albeit never one uttered in Marcy's presence.

On that front, her neighbours recognized early she needed some assistance getting through life. How she'd made it this far none knew — other than learning she was in her early forties, related to the Fergusons, and her deceased husband's name was Oliver, they knew nothing of her background. "But this is now," as Pam explained to Roger, and soon enough she got Marcy to move into a bedroom apartment in their Toronto house. In addition, they began delivering her to and from Whisper, saving her from the bus she took her first several trips.

It was George Clarke, however, who most tucked Marcy under a wing when it came to Whisper Island. Seeing her cottage slowly falling into disrepair he assumed the task of maintaining it. Indeed, within a year of Marcy's arrival he was spending more time working on her place than on his own. His neighbours, mind you, questioned some of his proclaimed "critical" chores, teasingly citing romantic interests as the true motive for his visits to Marcy. But regardless, his efforts were greatly appreciated, and did not go unrecognized.

About seven one summer evening, right after he'd finished his supper, George heard footsteps on his deck. Lots of footsteps. And before he reached his door, it was opened for him. "Surprise!" Pam and Marcy sang out in unison. So began "a belated" cottage warming, the island's fourth and final.

The group played cards, drank, and generally carried on at length that evening. The booze helped George loosen up and eventually he talked as much as anyone. In years following, it should be noted, he would find this 'help' no longer necessary.

It was about midnight that Pam slipped outside a moment. Returning with a small, neatly wrapped present, she handed it to George. Smiling but also eyeing him, she said, "No arguments: go on and open that puppy."

Since she'd stared him down before, George slowly opened the gift. Turned out it was a small plaque; a rough pine base sporting a brass plate. George read the engraving aloud.

'Whispered' Greetings!
A cottage tended,
The neighbours befriended,
Now you're ready for AA meetings!

As Pam so hoped, laughter followed, and the evening nicely came to a close. What became of the silly plaque thereafter none of George's fellow islanders knew, but all felt it had served its purpose. George Clarke was now officially a member of the family.

With Whisper's community now complete, and George not fearing a bad apple might yet enter the barrel, he increasingly settled into his cottage neighbourhood. As you will soon see, those neighbours would also slowly settle into him. With their bonding came the establishment of numerous island traditions, and one was having Thanksgiving supper together.

The Marsdens proposed and hosted the first event. This in 1976, only one year after Marcy joined Whisper. Somehow to all it seemed a fitting occasion to celebrate the cottaging season.

The islanders sat down to that first Thanksgiving supper about five on Sunday. "Duded up," George wore a thick, hand-knitted sweater (bought, as usual, at an auction) complete with a crooked bow tie. And so slick did he look that Roger soon suggested George offer the evening's toast. He did so jokingly, mind you. Somehow George didn't strike him as the 'toast type.'

But Roger had not finished chuckling when George, along with his back, rose. After gently clearing his throat, and after staring vacantly out the window half a minute, he at last spoke.

Well ... here the hell we are, sort of
Gettin' ready to eat all this stuff
Nice day for it, I guess
The fall leaves are ... comin' down

So, while everything's still hot
And nobody's, well, arguin' or nothing
We should maybe get at'er

That delivered, George raised his glass — alone.

Soon after, Roger burst out laughing. When Pam jabbed at him, he said, "But ... it's a joke, honey. You *are* making a joke — right, George? *Right?*"

George eyed him, sadly. "Somethin' more needs sayin'."

"No — nothing at all," Pam said before Roger could continue. With a warm smile she added, "That was very nice, George. A very nice toast to our beloved Whisper community. Cheers."

With that came the clinking of glasses.

4

"I'm really sorry, but it looks like we won't be up now until Saturday night," Pam Marsden explained to George by phone. "I've got a special doctor's appointment Friday evening, and Marcy's cousin Reed is visiting Saturday afternoon to discuss reunion plans."

"And Evan's not coming up *at all*, you say?"

"No. Some piece of machinery broke down at work and — this is a brave employer, I think — it seems Evan's been given the job of fixing it."

"Terrific."

It was the last Friday of June, 2002, and the start of a long weekend, courtesy of Canada Day falling on a Monday this year. Pam's message was delivered Thursday night while George was still in Whitby and he did not consider it good news. With all the vandalism on the island having been committed on Friday and Saturday nights, it was then the fort obviously needed most guarding. This particular Friday he would now be left alone to this task and it was one he didn't relish. A sleepless night patrolling the island, trying to protect all bases, undoubtedly lay ahead.

He considered himself lucky, however, anytime he arrived at Ferg Landing to his boat still afloat, which it was.

So too its motor starting, which it did. All in all, then, cruising to the island just after noon this warm, bright day George convinced himself he'd become paranoid. Heck, the sun was shining, a pine-scented breeze was wafting through his hair, and his baby was carving the lake smooth as silk. When he arrived a beer was in order. "Whoopee-doodle," as one of his elderly city neighbours would say.

Sadly, such joviality didn't last long.

George spotted the severe lean to his cottage well before reaching his dock. Within about thirty seconds he viewed it much closer, almost putting *The Pride of Whisper* up on his dock in the process. He also as quickly confirmed his suspected reason for the lean.

Someone had kindly removed — entirely — the pier blocks under his cottage's northernmost corner. In addition to other serious damage, the resulting sag was more than enough to shatter his bedroom window. And having observed all this, it was perhaps just as well George was alone on the island: his subsequent outburst could have been likened to a tempest.

He had needed this weekend, he told himself repeatedly while soon sitting at his kitchen table, tossing back several scotches with a hand still trembling. This was not how it was supposed to play out; cottaging was supposed to be relaxing, something helping you recover from life's ordeals — especially the sort of work week he'd been through. Not only did he now face replacing a window but he knew other repairs would be worse. He had long suffered problems with his cottage foundation and adjustments always meant considerable time and aggravation. Without a doubt, most if not all his much-needed weekend was about to dissolve.

Unfortunately, what he discovered next on this day only further dampened his spirits. Upon entering the cottage he

initially kept to the kitchen, which was kitty-corner to his
ailing bedroom. At last, however, he rose from his chair and
gently made his approach.

The bedroom was in shambles; even worse than he had
feared. Along with the smashed window, much of the tongue
and groove pine on the walls was split or entirely broken.
Half the ceiling tiles had come down, and his dresser had
toppled forward, leaving its shattered mirror scattered over
the bed.

But George's attention soon focused on a comparatively
small item he noticed. The plaque he'd received at his
housewarming so many years back now lay on the floor,
badly marked and broken in two by the falling dresser.
Stooping, he picked up the remains and studied them.
"Fixable," he quickly assured himself. Nonetheless he
continued staring at the broken plaque nearly a minute.

Within half an hour he set to work repairing the
foundation. He began by donning ancient coveralls smeared
with "oil, paint, and God only knows," and sporting several
pairs of old underwear hanging from the pockets to serve as
rags. He then assembled spare pier blocks (the originals had
apparently gone for a swim), wood scraps to act as shims, and
assorted hand tools. Relatively speaking he made good
progress with these preparations. Soon after starting the job
of lifting the cottage's corner, however, he discovered his
hydraulic jack was not working. From ageing or perhaps for
some other reason (about which he wondered), the "stupid,
bloody jack" wouldn't hold any pressure.

Defeated, he could only grab his keys and wallet and
head for the dock.

'Kirkdale's GotItAll' was a veritable institution on Green Heron. By 2002 Howard and Rose Kirkdale had operated the combination general store, garage, and gas station thirty-four years. As the store's name implied, you could buy, rent, or 'short-term swipe' most anything here. In their tiny garage Howard and his long-time mechanic Arnold Knapp could also seemingly repair any object in the known universe. Kirkdale's was thus a bustling place during cottage season, and how "seventy-something or other" Howard and Rose still kept a handle on everything seemed to most a minor miracle.

So well did George know the store's hardware section, when he arrived he quickly found a new jack. Paying took longer; when he reached the front counter he met Howard amid conversation.

"I can get one in for you soon, though," the silver-haired storekeeper apologetically offered a short, burly man George knew was a building contractor. "Last Saturday one of my regulars bought the only one I had in stock."

The builder rubbed his forehead. "Thanks, but the client wants this job finished and done with this weekend. I'll have to whip over and grab one in Birchport."

"You're sure the rig you've got is toast? Arnie might be able to do a number on it for you."

"I realize, but — no offence, Howard — by the time you pay someone to fix a come-along you may as well buy a new one. But thanks again." With that the contractor bid his adieu.

By this time others were in line behind George so he could only trade quick hellos, pay for the jack, and step out. This frustrated him; in private he would have tried learning, uninclined to gossip as Mr. Kirkdale might be, just who it was that bought the store's last hand winch. His mind was now churning.

He did have another option for gaining the desired data, however, and that was through Howard's mechanic. When not busy in the garage Arnold Knapp often helped in the store and therefore might know about the winch. He also wasn't known for driving the quickest racecar on the track, and so he might just be, George contemplated, a touch easier to 'milk.'

He found the gangly, coveralled mechanic cleaning his hands in the garage's hopelessly grungy sink. After politely offering one of his retired pairs of underwear as a towel, and Arnold graciously accepting, George sighed and said, "Looks like I'm out of luck today. Came in for a new come-along, but seems you're fresh out."

Arnold first silently offered his standard gaze, which bore a curious mix of innocence and suspicion. Tapping his cigarette ash in the sink he then asked, "Takin' out a stump or somethin', are you George?"

The stump remover nodded. "You boys wouldn't have a come-along I could steal for an afternoon, would you?"

"Nope. 'Fraid ours are all tied up slingin' woodies. Not one to spare."

George predicted this answer; among their myriad services the Kirkdales launched and lifted boats. Before launching wooden boats they were typically slung partially in the water to allow their hulls to soak up and seal. With plenty customers this naturally required many winches.

"Know of anyone, then, that might lend me theirs? Maybe ... the fella that bought your last, by chance?"

Arnold chortled. "That was Stan Milne, so I doubt he'd help you out." Coughing and cracking up altogether, the mechanic added, "More likely to winch you into a tree, Georgie!"

George might have joined in this laugh, but the name Stan Milne now made his mind churn even more. A hunch soon followed.

Quickly returning to Whisper, George immediately inspected again his cottage's ailing corner. As he suspected, no evidence existed of someone raising the cottage to remove the pier blocks; a base for the jack, for instance, would surely have left a footprint. Next he studied nearby trees, looking for tell-tale marks. Sure enough, a large maple bore scars from a chain. "The bugger just *pulled* the stupid pier out," George whispered, shaking his head in disbelief. Dropped so quickly, no wonder the cottage was so badly damaged.

By this time George had no doubts about who the "bugger" was. For one, Stan Milne just happened to have bought himself a new come-along. As for the boldness of buying his weapon so close to home, Stan was more than bold enough; Lord, George had seen plenty of that side of him. Stan was also fully aware of how tedious it was to raise George's cottage by jack. After all, in his past schemings had he not repeatedly mentioned as much?

When the Fergusons put Whisper up for sale in 1973 they were not exactly bombarded with offers. As mentioned, few on Green Heron saw much appeal to the island. One cottager that did was Stan Milne, a retired mason, but he happened to be in Florida when the Fergusons listed the island lots. By a margin of several days George closed on the island's northwest property before Stan could offer a superior bid.

Not interested in the island's larger and more expensive lots, this caused Mr. Milne great frustration and he paid regular visits to the new islander before, during, and after he built his cottage. Such calls were clearly in the interest of buying George out, and all manner of offers were delivered. He also brought George's attention to a host of problems with the island lot, including how troublesome a foundation would prove.

To all this George nodded at regular intervals but ultimately did not budge, and predictably relations between him and Stan soon became decidedly sour. Despite pleas for peace from Mary Milne, who apparently did not bear any grudge against George, rarely did either of the men mention the other's name now without harsh words attached.

Accordingly fired up and braced for battle, George boated to Stan Milne's cottage within fifteen minutes of discovering the chain scars on his maple. The motive and evidence were all there, he assured himself; he needed no further convincing.

The Milnes were on Franklin, a large, granite-domed island in Green Heron's northwestern corner. Perched on a treacherously steep lot and sporting shallow and weedy frontage their cottage had never appealed to George. Nor evidently anyone else; for decades Stan and Mary had tried unsuccessfully to sell. George thus understood perfectly why Stan desired a cottage elsewhere, and also why his offers for a certain Whisper lot had been conditional. What George *didn't* understand was why Stan bought this lousy lot in the first place, and why the heck someone else should bear the brunt of the mistake. Go whoopee-doodle yourself, mister.

After docking George headed up immediately to the Milnes' small, "puke-green" cottage. Albeit fuming he ascended the steep path slowly, determined to refrain from attacking immediately. During the boat trip he decided he'd first poke at Stan a bit, see if he could rattle him and cause a slip.

He quickly spotted his prey, hoeing as it was in a vegetable garden. Tall and stocky (and large-footed, George soon confirmed), Stan Milne was by no means a small man, but that along with brandishing a garden hoe wouldn't save him. Neither, George decided, would his fifteen additional years or bad back; all sympathies had been forfeited.

"Well! Good day, Mr. Clarke!" Stan offered by way of his now standard sarcastic tone with George. "Long time no see."

"Yes, it's been a while. I don't see near as much of you as I used to. Funny how that is."

To this Stan stopped work and for a moment eyed George, who was now within twenty feet. He then slowly resumed his labours and calmly said, "So what brings you to our fine abode? Can I offer you a thirst-quencher?"

"Thanks, but no — I only came to see if you might be kind enough to lend me a jack, being the good buddy you arc. Mine seems to be on the fritz."

"I would — very obviously, George — but I'm afraid that's something I don't have."

George wanted to counter with, "Yeah, I know you bloody well don't," but instead sighed and delivered, "That's a darn shame. I guess I'll have to live with walking uphill every morning when I get out of bed."

He studied Stan closely, watching his eyes; George had already learned from past experience Stan wasn't a good liar. But without the slightest hint of nervousness the Franklin islander responded with, "Sorry? Walk uphill?"

George continued staring at Stan a moment, then said,

"Guess you're not aware. I've suffered a major setback with my cottage. Seems one corner's sittin' kind of low on account of nothing holding that corner up anymore."

Once again in routine tone, Stan said, "You don't say? Oh my goodness!"

"Now maybe it was the local wildlife; I don't know — do porcupines chew at cement blocks just like they do at plywood? Or then again, maybe a defunct Russian satellite came spiralling out of orbit and ran smack dab into that pier." Once more looking at Stan directly, George added, "But then again, I'm thinking maybe the source of the problem was a touch more familiar, and say ... predictable."

Stan's eyes lit up. "Oh, I see. *Yours truly* did it."

George was through with subtleties; adopting a grave, snarling voice he let loose. "You just can't accept defeat, can you? Didn't get the lot you wanted and now you're out to wreck it for me and — why not — the other islanders as well. Little bloody crybaby."

Stan scoffed. "Have you lost your min—?"

"I know you bought a come-along from Howard last Saturday, and you're just the bloody type to pull a stunt like this. And all the other little stunts we've suffered on the island the last few seasons. You've been having yourself a veritable field day with us, haven't you?"

George's face was now fiery red. Stan's, however, was decidedly not so. Very calmly, and accompanied by only a mischievous grin, he delivered, "Only one little problem with your theory, Georgie ol' boy."

"Yeah? And what the friggin' heck is that?"

"Mary and I stayed in Florida until mid-June this year, and right after one weekend here — last weekend — we visited Mary's family in London for a week. Only flew back across the big pond yesterday. So it would have been quite a trick for me to do these 'stunts', as you call them. Sorry to break all this to you."

"Sure about that story, Stan? A guy can easily check on these things."

Pointing to Mary, who had come out to the cottage's front porch, Stan said, "Go right ahead."

Bubbly-faced as usual with George, Mary yelled, "Hello, love! How are things? Can I get you tea, or something cold?"

"Thanks but no thanks," George politely replied, then fearing (knowing) the answer but pathetically proceeding anyway, he asked, "How was Florida and the motherland, Mary?"

"Both lovely. Absolutely charming. You'll have to come in sometime and see our pictures. My goodness, we haven't chatted in a while."

When George turned back to Stan he saw a predictably smug grin. "You're barking up the wrong tree, Clarke. Now, if you don't mind, I really should get back to work. I'm sure a genius like you can find his own way down to the dock."

"I can find my own bloody way to the cop station, too," George countered, but very feebly, as he started toward his boat.

"Once again," Stan offered smartly, "go right ahead."

After that confrontation George stewed at length. *Seemingly* he may have been mistaken about Stan, but he was by no means entirely convinced. That thinking changed, however, when he raised the issue with Roger after he, Pam, and Marcy arrived at the island Saturday evening. He made his trip to the Marsdens about nine and not long after he finally finished work resurrecting his cottage.

"He picked up the come-along at Kirkdale's for a friend, George," Roger sympathetically explained while chaining up his boat. "I'm sure because I helped the friend use it last weekend. As for the Milnes being away, I could have told you that too." Soon he ended with, "I'm sorry, but you've seriously jumped the gun here."

For George the news was the knockout blow; he was now in, as he put such predicaments, "a doozy of a wiggle." What he did next he found rather unpleasant, but his principled nature forced.

The following Sunday morning, right after spending nearly two hours glueing back together a certain plaque, he returned to Stan Milne's place and apologized.

Granted it was not lengthy nor particularly overflowing with emotion, but it was an apology nonetheless. And Stan, bless his heart, was good about it: he only smirked twice and snickered once.

5

On an early October day in 1874 a tired canoe sank near Whisper Island. An equally tired pioneer made it ashore but thereupon was stranded. No one had yet settled on Green Heron, meaning his shouts for help went unanswered, and he feared a mainland swim too cool and lengthy. Seemingly he could only wait, hoping another settler knew of the lake's abundant trout.

Halbert Desmond — thirty, straggly-haired, newly thin — had been in Canada only eighteen months. Lured by free land he and his wife had emigrated from Boston. The couple had been eager, even brazen while sharing with parents and friends their grand plans. This despite hearing farming was especially difficult in this rock-infested region of Ontario, and despite knowing nothing of wilderness life. Halbert could now only begrudgingly admit problems and setbacks already numbered many. Pathetically losing his rickety, overloaded canoe to a sharp rock was merely the latest.

It was late afternoon and he had intended to camp soon at a familiar mainland site. This small island he had previously given little consideration, so uninviting seemed its tangle of tree and rock. Apparently it would now suffice, and with darkness rapidly approaching and no help in sight he set about collecting deadwood for a fire. Swimming ashore he succeeded in towing his pack, and contents included wooden matches sealed in a bottle.

He landed on a long point of exposed bedrock, and in gathering firewood he stayed close to this natural clearing. The woods were steadily darkening and he'd been blessed with many a story of what could befall an unarmed soul in the bush at night. He longed for his rifle, which now lay on the lake's bottom.

In less than fifteen minutes he managed a small fire. Removing his soaked shirt and trousers he draped each over a dead birch branch he pinched upright with several large stones. Soon his body was dry but despite this and the warmth of the fire he found himself still shivering. Beyond the circle of firelight the nearby woods were now engulfed in blackness, and to his nervous ears came the various calls and rustlings of the forest night.

During these hours he thought of Boston, longingly, and similarly of his dear young wife. She at least would not yet be worrying; he was on merely the first day of an intended week long hunting and fishing trip. He also felt confident that if he perished his neighbouring homesteaders, who had proved so kind and helpful, would take Gilda under their wing. Or perhaps she would somehow return to Boston and escape altogether this hell of rock, stump, and bug. He and Gilda had already discussed this several times under the guise of kidding, but increasingly it made sense. What point existed in stubbornly trying to survive this nightmare? He saw no loss in abandoning a muddy, flea-infested cabin, nor the several cleared acres pathetically posing as farmland. As for this never-ending, unforgiving, Godforsaken bush — the ultimate source of their misery — they certainly would not miss it either.

Halbert pined as such right into his sleep, which did

finally come through sheer fatigue. Now dressed again and laying on mud-padded bedrock with his pack for a pillow, his last movement was to draw his hands into his sleeves, and his last image was of what seemed an especially indifferent star-filled sky.

The following morning he woke with a start. Turning toward a curious chattering he saw a black-masked face, and two piercing eyes.

The raccoon seemed unconcerned with his awakening. Twisting its head it stared at the newcomer a moment, quizzically, then resumed chewing at his pack. At some point in the night Halbert had either pushed his pillow aside, or someone presently nearby had pulled it.

"Shoo!" Halbert yelled. "Get on with you!"

Not until he rose did the raccoon retreat, and then only slowly and offering several vicious growls. Ambling along shore it soon unsuccessfully pursued a frog, then overturned a small rock in the shallows to probe for crayfish, also without luck. All clearly in the interest of a bedtime snack, but it soon stopped and peered a moment at a maple sapling in an inspective manner, seemingly judging the young tree's worthiness. Halbert watched the lordly, nocturnal animal continue as such until rounding a corner and leaving his view.

He was relieved to find his provisions unharmed. Also he was amazed he wasn't bitten; in the mud around where he slept were many hand-like prints. Halbert surmised the raccoon had even sniffed his face several times.

It was still very early — just after dawn — and for a moment he watched mist float over the lake's shiny surface. He then stretched, trying to relieve the stiffness in his back, and again lit a small fire, this time for coffee. While heating a tiny pot of lake water he also partook in several biscuits Gilda had provisioned him with. Having salvaged his pack from the previous day's disaster meant food would not be a critical problem — at least for a week. As he ate he assured himself his predicament would not last longer.

With breakfast complete he donned his pack and began walking along shore, heading the same direction as his early visitor. He would circle the island such that he could scan the lake and mainland in all directions. Surely help would eventually appear.

At this southern end of the island two points stretched some hundred yards into Green Heron. Halbert had come ashore and camped on the westernmost. When he reached the eastern point, whose sharp, offshore boulders initiated his canoe's demise, he spat on the bedrock at his feet. He'd be quite content, he considered, if never in his life seeing another rock.

Upon rounding this point he gained a view of the eastern mainland, and to his chagrin saw no signs of anyone. He stood gazing several minutes before resuming his shoreline tour.

Although including scattered maples and birches, the island's forest was dominated by young white spruces. Loggers had harvested the giant white pines ruling during pre-settlement times. But the island was quickly recovering and its woods were already thick. Even with autumn and many of the trees' leaves having fallen, Halbert could not see far through them.

When reaching the island's northern end he found both

surprise and opportunity. Here several acres of fractured and boulder-riddled bedrock rose steeply from the water. Not only did this barren headland offer Halbert relief from the forest, but also a commanding view.

He was still panting from the climb when he once again felt disappointment in his search for help. As broad as the headland's view was, it offered not even a hint of fellow settlers or their trappings. Sweeping the mainland woods he saw only several ducks winging along shore, and on the smooth lake only this vista brightly mirrored.

Merely the island's western view remained, and Halbert's optimism was dwindling. Something he did gain from the headland, however, was sight of an even better lookout. Behind him, a white pine on the island's western side was curiously spared by loggers, and from this tall tree he could perhaps see beyond Green Heron's shoreline forest to a settler's clearing. A waving torch at night might then prove his saviour.

Quickly descending the granite headland he made his way along the western shore. As he had worried he saw nothing from lake level providing hope, but he now felt sure the white pine would deliver. At a trot he reached it in only a few minutes.

At its base the pine was some three feet in diameter — by no means large compared to former neighbours — and Halbert quickly saw why loggers neglected it. Crooked, gnarled, and split-trunked it would have provided little and poor lumber. Ironically, for Halbert an early division in the trunk offered an easy first perch, and from there he could reach abundant branches for climbing.

The pine did indeed offer an impressive view of the mainland, and for once Halbert could see it in all directions. He was even able to gaze northeast to the meandering inlet creek by which he had entered the lake. Other than this treeless channel, however, the forest canopy was unbroken and stretched forever. Studying the view for some fifteen minutes he saw no settler's clearing. Depressed more than ever, he slowly descended.

As though his spirits needed further dampening, Halbert's hands slipped on one of the tree's moist, lowermost branches. He fell only perhaps ten feet but his right foot landed on one of the pine's protruding roots and turned slightly. Circling the tree, hobbling in pain, he worried his predicament had seriously worsened.

He spent the afternoon soaking his ankle in the lake, groaning, and stewing. Sinister thoughts included burning the nearby pine down, and perhaps the whole pathetic island forest. But in time he cooled off and regained basic sense, and when darkness approached he simply lit a small fire as he had the previous evening.

He at least prepared a better bed his second night. Using his hunting knife he cut several dozen spruce bows and these he wove into two crude blankets. One he lay beneath him and one over. He also braved a wooded resting place high on shore, near the big pine, where a patch of bedrock sported thick moss.

Although more comfortable he still struggled getting to sleep that evening, mulling over as he did the day's events. And of course, an aching ankle was no help.

After breakfast the following morning Halbert once again started the day with a shoreline scan of the mainland.

Although still sore, his ankle luckily was well enough to permit walking.

He had awoken to birdsong — a soft medley of chirps and trills — and he was not long in discovering the resident musicians. In a spruce-rich cove farther south along the western shore he came across goldfinches — dozens of them. As Halbert walked through their home the birds dipped and wove around and over him, tiny bursts of bright yellow amid the dark greens of the spruces.

Soon after leaving the birds Halbert encountered an old friend: the island's king, touring his minions. 'His Raccoonship,' as Halbert decided he should be dubbed, was once again leaving no article unpursued or uninspected as he circled the palace grounds. He granted another growl when he saw the strange, two-legged creature had not yet departed his island. "Show me a way and I'll be gone," the two-legger offered, even smiling a moment.

The remainder of the island's west side was the last of the shoreline Halbert had not yet seen, and it initially revealed little of interest. Just before returning to his landing point, however, he came across a fallen birch, and with it gained an idea: if he could drag the small tree into the water, holding it he might dog paddle to the mainland.

The plan proved hopeless. Not only did his sore ankle make getting the tree into the lake exceedingly difficult and tiresome, once there it barely floated, so quickly did the pulpy wood soak up water. And when he tried dog paddling with the tree the lake was cool enough to make his teeth chatter after he'd journeyed only several hundred feet from shore. Disgusted, he abandoned the birch and swam back, plunked his soaked and shivering body down on a sun-warmed rock, and simply gazed into the blue of the sky an hour. Eventually he considered taking a stab at the mainland without a float, and drown if need be, but like his island-burning notion better sense prevailed.

By the time he resigned entirely from his swimming scheme mid-afternoon had arrived. Exhausted, Halbert decided to consume the remainder of the day resting and considering new approaches to self-rescue. This effort did not bear fruit, however, and left him depressed and muttering to himself. It also planted the first seeds of worry: would he indeed escape this newfound hell? He began wondering.

In days following Halbert made no further attempts at self-rescue. Along with lacking new ideas, he decided he was endangering himself unnecessarily. Merely a day's paddle from his homestead and those of many others, surely someone would venture this way soon enough. And upon rescue, having an injury — such as the broken ankle he'd nearly suffered — would obviously be a serious hindrance over the upcoming winter. So, heeding surely his father's words of advice, he would "exercise some patience."

Halbert thus continued circling the island several times a day to scan the lake and mainland, but now did so in a more relaxed manner. Nursing a still tender ankle, he frequently stopped during these tours, finding a log, rock, or leafy slope at the forest's edge upon which to settle himself.

This daily routine obviously offered Halbert considerable time for contemplation, and potentially for worry. Again disciplining himself, he resolved not to fret over his present predicament. There was Gilda to consider, for instance; how she had been so strong through their recent ordeals, how he in turn had drawn from that strength. In this same light he also pondered how generous their fellow homesteaders had been of both Gilda and himself. They might still decide to leave Canada, but that decision surely would have come much sooner without the aid and support they'd received. Indeed, if anything enticed them to remain it would be the warmth of this settlement community. "One draws strength from bonds of all manner and origin," he recalled his grandfather once contending, and he now knew this to be true.

Ironically, Halbert's attention also turned to that which his bonds helped him struggle against. This opponent, of course, was everywhere around him. How many trees such as those on the island had he cut down? How many rocks like those scattered along its shore had he moved or buried? Yet much of what he began noticing on the island during his lengthy tours was, curiously, quite new to him. Although since arriving from Boston he'd been immersed in endless wilds, he'd never truly studied them. Not, at least, in any other than a practical vein. He had studied trees, for example, but only in judging them as obstacles to be cleared, lumber, firewood, or, as it went, watchtowers. All understandable consequences, Halbert supposed, of desperately hacking out a life in the wilderness. But now, for once freed of his considerable toils, he found himself considering his woodsy surroundings in a different and rather curious light.

One of the first things on the island catching Halbert's attention was, oddly enough, a large toad. He came across this peculiar resident during his fourth morning. Seconds after seating himself on a moss-covered log on the eastern shore the toad crawled out from under a mat of fall leaves.

Watching the pudgy, 'wart'-studded creature, Halbert reflected on how it too was effectively imprisoned on the island. At one point facing his fellow inmate, the toad's wry expression even seemed to suggest this. "Yes, we're two peas in a pod, we are," Halbert said aloud, chuckling.

By now he had already seen many birds on or around the island. Besides the ducks he spotted in flight during his first headland visit, he came across many others swimming along the island's shallows. These were almost entirely common mergansers. Halbert marvelled at how gracefully these birds paddled about and dove in search of food. With their orange bills, crested reddish brown heads, and well-preened silvery white feathers he also found them rather handsome. In time he delighted in being able to view them quite close, the birds gradually growing accustomed to his presence.

Naturally Halbert also continued waking to the songs of the goldfinches. Instead of immediately rising as he had the first morning hearing them, he now remained in his spruce bed for a spell, listening. Sometimes he even tried mimicking their canarylike chirps and twitters. After rising he would pay a visit to their little cove, and always he would become mesmerized by the speed and agility of their flights. At no time, though, did Halbert sense the birds were distressed by his presence; rather, they seemed as curious about him as he was of them.

Not only did the island's fauna attract Halbert's attention during his tours, but also its trees and plants. Upon sitting at the forest's edge one afternoon he was treated to the scent of wild mint. On another the bright orange of jewelweed flowers caught his eye. And during all stops Halbert came to enjoy watching yellow and red autumn leaves descend in twists and turns from surrounding trees. He became particularly curious, however, about the western shore's giant pine. Setting aside earlier grievances, Halbert was awed by the tenacity of this badly blemished tree. It had apparently overcome all manner of hardships, including what appeared a lightning strike near its top.

Lastly, the island's headland became for Halbert a favourite spot. Not only did it offer a broad view of the northern mainland but also a welcome breeze. The week had been unseasonably warm, and Halbert much enjoyed a soft, fresh wind that always blew in from the northwest starting about mid-morning. While seated here Halbert also made a study of the headland's broad expanse of granite, which dipped steeply into the lake. Running his hands over the sun warmed rock he came to feel comfort in the island's rugged and seemingly indestructible foundation, sunken canoes forgiven.

All these experiences Halbert ultimately digested while laying in his bed at night. Just before sunset every day he would light a small fire on shore to cook his supper, then retire to his bed of spruce blankets. Luckily the weather remained clear during his stay on the island, and so each night he was greeted by a sky rich with stars.

It was then he would recount his day's activities and, always, wonder at his changing feelings toward his island 'hell.' Somehow, both consciously and unconsciously, it had chipped away at his bitterness. So too his fears; he no longer trembled at night, and sounds around him even became somewhat soothing.

Eventually he was reminded of a conversation the previous winter with another settler, one older and more seasoned.

"A traditional native doesn't see things the same as us blokes," the British man explained, huddled in front of Halbert's woodstove. "For him the woods aren't an enemy to defeat but a brother to help and be helped by. The land itself he sees as a member of his community. That's why I think the natives find our word 'wild' rather odd; it implies a separation, and they simply don't see one."

Like so much else, the settler's message became lost for Halbert in the blur of building his farm. Indeed, he recalled nodding off to sleep not long after this talk. Yet now, able to think as clearly as he had before emigrating, he could not deny merit to this message. Perhaps, in the end, it was like his grandfather had said, "One draws strength from bonds of all manner and origin."

This realization perhaps came to him most powerfully his fifth evening on the island. By his instincts he judged he'd been in bed an hour when behind him he heard a rustling sound. Turning, he peered into the moonlit forest. Soon enough he discerned a familiar shape, and also a familiar bold disposition.

"Yes, my lord — still part of the family," he offered as his majesty coolly ambled past.

He uttered the words in jest, but somehow they remained with him long afterward, echoing. Indeed, they lingered right into his sleep, which on this night came peacefully, and soundly.

Like his first, Halbert woke with a start his sixth island morning.

But this time it was a voice.

Quickly pushing aside his blanket of spruce bows he rolled onto his side to see two burly men in a small skiff. By

their similar appearance Halbert guessed them father and
son, and by their fishing gear also guessed their mission.
From the elder of the two came, "I said — is you stuck?"

Soon after, Halbert left Whisper Island. He sat in the
bow, politely entertaining questions from his rescuers and
nodding at their various speculations. "Lucky a bear didn' git
you," the rowing son observed, while the father, studying a
splintered gunnel, asked, "You lookin' now to buy another
boat, mister?"

Mostly Halbert gazed back at the receding island. The
breeze from the northwest had commenced and for a
moment he could still watch leaves slowly descending from
the headland's birches. When these faded several mergansers
caught his attention, and in turn the swaying crown of the
island's tenacious big pine. And once quite distant from the
island he simply imagined it; smiling within, he even
considered a certain amphibian friend, one undoubtedly
curious about his release.

Feeling they would expect it, to his companions Halbert
gruffly declared, "Suppose in the end the place didn't get the
better of me." Then at last he turned to face ahead to the
approaching mainland — to a beloved wife, to a farm, and to
perhaps a home.

6

Atop a patch of mossy bedrock near Whisper's aged pine, a great blue heron studied at length that even greater blue spread before it. Its gazing eyes glowed the same saffron yellow of the late sun, which neared the trees of the distant mainland. Seemingly inspired it at last spread its wings and rose into the evening air, freshly tracing the shoreline before passing the island's southwest point, where Whisper's foundation slowly dipped beneath the lake's now glassy surface.

And where Evan Dean stood watching.

Seated in an Adirondack chair on the Marsdens' spacious front deck, a smiling Marcy Willett said to Pam, "you're a treat," before accepting a glass of iced tea. Seated in a matching chair beside her George Clarke sipped at a beer, while Roger Marsden, the cook of the evening, tended a barbecue laden with baking apples. Evan, as mentioned, stood alone near shore.

"You're missing it," George yelled to the island's youngest cottager, referring to the scent of cinnamon emanating from the barbecue.

"He's having a philosophical moment — leave him," said Pam. "He needs his philosophical moments."

"What our blonde buddy needs is a replacement chip

and a higher-voltage battery," Roger countered, and with a chortle George nodded.

Following a tradition established even earlier than their Saturday breakfast gatherings, the islanders were now gathered and taking in the evening's sunset. With a perfect, unobstructed view from their west-facing front deck the Marsdens always played host to these occasions. This especially thrilled Pam; nothing in this world did she enjoy more than a party, even if only a small one.

Like all parties large and small, silliness was invariably a guest at what were dubbed "sunsetters." Roger returned bare-footed from the kitchen one evening to find the toes of his old deck slippers filled with mink droppings; his feet were all but home when Evan's sudden grin tipped him off. Another evening water-ballooning hosts soaked both George and Marcy to the bone. On yet another Evan had to swim home when his trunks parted his body as he dove from the Marsdens' dock; for that he had Pam and a fishing rod to thank. The list goes on. Regardless of the day's or week's events, and regardless of whether the sunset was even visible, the islanders often congregated at the Marsdens' in early evening for a drink and a laugh.

These informal meetings did, however, have other and more serious functions. For one, through Roger's initiative the cottagers established in 1986 an island fund, and it was at meetings they made decisions regarding communal spending. More important, it was here any and all grievances among islanders were worked out. If Evan was playing his stereo too loud, he was politely informed. If George was exhibiting one too many yard sale masterpieces outside the main gallery, he was ribbed accordingly. "You nip neighbourly problems in the bud; you don't wait until hating him or her before raising issue," was how Roger described this thinking, and all islanders would surely have agreed. Meetings thus proved quite beneficial in the pursuit of island peace.

The practical component of 'sunsetters' was very much prevalent this Friday evening in mid-July, several weeks following George's misadventure with Stan Milne. With this disaster, and no further clues in sight, a "major powwow" was clearly in order.

"It seems we're all agreed now the Dempster boys aren't who we're after," Roger began when Evan at last rejoined the group. "That means we need to adjust our sights; keep our eyes open for a man working alone rather than a couple of kids."

"And a man with big feet," added Pam.

"Yes, and that's no joke," Roger continued. "If anyone spots someone at Kirkdale's or in Birchport wearing a pair of snowshoes, try finding out who they are, silly as that might seem. You could even watch where they walk and get a look at their shoe or boot prints. I took pictures of the prints George found, so we could compare."

"Anybody with feet that big should be arrested anyway," said George.

Evan now slyly asked, "During this morning's outing did you happen to notice any *more* prints, George?"

His neighbour sneered. "Oh, I saw prints all right, smarty."

Pam said, "What's this?"

"I forgot to tell you, hon," Roger cut in. "Our neighbour had his favourite visitor drop by again this morning."

George said, "I woke up early as usual, and made the mistake of stepping out for some air."

Pam smiled. "And someone was there to say hello?"

"Wanted to talk at length, it seemed, but I declined the

offer, unsociable as that may have been."

Roger said, "But at least you ran for *your* cottage — right, George?" and this sparked a round of laughter.

Roger was referring to an encounter George had several years earlier. Immediately after rising Mr. Clarke hastily made a trip to his shed for tools to fix a leaking bathroom pipe. He'd just come out of the shed when he was startled by a black bear near his side door, blocking his path. Worse, the large animal ambled toward him and he had no choice but to slowly retreat along one of the island's interior paths. Eventually, in fact, he retreated all the way to the Marsdens. So it happened that Pam opened her living room drapes that morning to warm sun, hummingbirds at her window feeder, and George Clarke streaking onto her deck in only his underwear.

"But now in all seriousness," Roger said when the group had quieted again, "everybody needs to keep their eyes open. We need to nail this bugger. Marcy's reunion isn't that far off and we obviously don't want it ... well, *tampered with*."

Glancing at Marcy, who looked ill over this suggested possibility, Pam said, "She also obviously doesn't need any more stones in her bedroom."

"Yes, this is true," said Roger.

"That's why Marcy and I have decided to take matters into our own hands. The whole stones-in-the-bedroom thing has pushed us over the top. No creep is getting away with that."

Eyebrows high, Roger said, "Excuse me? You're taking what —?"

"Marcy and I have received a prime tip, and we've decided it's high time the gals of the island had a crack at solving our problems — right, Marcy?"

As Marcy nodded Roger stepped away from the

barbecue and stood immediately in front of Pam. "So what's this tip?"

"We'll be keeping that to ourselves for now, thanks."

Waving his tongs toward the mainland, Roger said, "Hunting this bugger down is no joke, you know. It could be dangerous." Glancing at George, who already knew what was coming, he added, "We also can't afford any more false accusations. We'll have the whole lake on our case if we keep that up."

Pam, however, remained firm. "Relax. You clearly underestimate us."

The 'gals' left for the mainland about ten the following bright morning. Their destination, which Pam refused to reveal to a highly annoyed husband, was nearly forty minutes away by boat. They therefore decided to simply dock at Ferg Landing and take Pam's car.

Over the years Marcy had paid countless visits to Gloria Shelborne. Both were 'gardenaholics' and could, as Pam knew well, discuss their mutual passion ad nauseum. Pam had, however, become acquainted with "Garden Gloria" only through her visits to Whisper; anytime Marcy had returned those visits, Pam merely dropped her at Kirkdale's. From there Gloria's husband, Quentin, drove Marcy the remaining miles.

Pam was thus not familiar with the route to the Shelborne cottage, and now at the mercy of Marcy's navigational skills. But the driver was determined not to allow this circumstance to worry her. She even found amusement in "the mercy of Marcy." Indeed she uttered this little tongue twister in her head repeatedly as they negotiated a maze of dusty cottage laneways.

By Pam's estimate they had driven about halfway when Marcy delivered a major confidence-booster. Pointing to her right, toward a tidy red cottage, she said, "Oh look! Stephanie bought the new planters. Aren't they beautiful?" Later came, "The Morgans have painted! What a lovely blue!" All was therefore well, and Pam scolded herself for being paranoid.

But then came — as Pam supposed the cottage road Gods must have deemed fitting — the dead end.

Marcy's reaction was predictable. "These trees were certainly not here last time!" After Pam turned the car around she was also not surprised that certain earlier landmarks were now viewed in a different light. "But ... that couldn't have been the Morgans' — their place is *two* storys! Oh my goodness!"

Pam spent the next half hour stubbornly searching — to no avail — and ultimately even got lost backtracking to Kirkdale's. Soon enough she began using language her passenger deemed "alarming." At last admitting defeat, she could only pull up to a cottage and call for help.

Wide-eyed, Marcy asked, "Are you sure they'll let you borrow their phone?"

Very wearily, Pam nodded. "They will because I'll be begging on my friggin' hands and knees."

As Pam exited the car and trudged to the cottage's door, Marcy leaned out the window and graciously offered, "Careful you don't dirty your slacks, dear."

They finally arrived at the Shelbornes' just after noon. A silver-haired, very full-figured Gloria, clad in sandals and a bright yellow shawl, greeted them in the driveway.

"I was getting so worried about you two! You must be exhausted — come in right away and I'll get you a drink. Oh, you poor things!"

That drink Pam would have greatly welcomed, but somehow twenty minutes passed before she received it. On their way inside Gloria felt inclined to present to her guests numerous flower gardens, and to hear their detailed appraisals (all from Marcy, and all smothered in "just delightfully wonderful!") Curiously, amid this tour Gloria also felt the islanders should be warned of "him," meaning her husband. Comments ranged from "Don't turn your back on *him*, whatever you do!" to "He's entirely worthless. How anyone should be expected to live with *him* is beyond me." All this Quentin either did not hear, or chose to disregard, because he merely continued with various chores about the yard.

Even once they were inside and the much-awaited drinks were delivered, Gloria kept conversation centred around the same two basic topics. At last, though, during a pause where both Gloria and Marcy simultaneously took sips from their drinks, Pam was able to jam a foot in the conversation's door.

As pleasantly and optimistically as she could manage at this point, Pam said, "So! I understand you have some important information for me, Gloria."

The host nodded. "Yes. I most certainly do." With that she began her presentation.

"A few days ago a dear friend of mine — who out of fear

for her life wishes to remain anonymous — told me she saw a man quickly boating away from Marcy's dock near dusk. This was back in early June. If you're wondering why the friend didn't tell me sooner it's because she wasn't aware of your vandalism problem until I happened to make mention. It was only several days ago, you see, she connected the two items."

Pam said, "It's okay — I understand. Did she get a good look at this man?"

"No, I'm afraid not. It was getting dark, remember. She could only see it was a big man, and that he seemed to be in a hurry. The situation struck her as a little odd because she knew Marcy wasn't up. This was the weekend she stayed in Toronto to work on her family reunion preparations."

"Which went well, by the way," Marcy piped in. "We got the musicians —"

"Hold the show!" Pam said this just a touch louder than she wanted to, and both her companions now wore startled faces.

"What's the matter, Pam?" Marcy softly asked.

Pulling somewhat on her own hair, Pam answered, "I'd like to just ... keep on track, if you don't mind." To Gloria she said, "So your friend has no idea who the man was?"

"Not even a hunch. And although after listening to her I clearly knew who it was, she still doesn't."

"Although *you* —?"

Gloria stared at Pam gravely. "This friend said the man in question was driving a pontoon boat, one with old tires for bumpers and a broken side railing. That's what tipped me off." With a sly squint Gloria strutted to her large front window, artfully fired back the drapes, and pointed. "Exactly like *that* pontoon boat right there."

Pam first stared in the direction of the Shelbornes' dock,

then at Gloria, quizzically. "But that's ... your boat."

"Yes, that's our boat." After glancing at Marcy for reassurance in proceeding, Gloria delivered in the severest tone, "It's my husband, *him*, who's been vandalizing your already haggard little island."

Seeing Marcy wore a similar severe expression and was nodding, Pam said, "Let me be clear on this. You're saying your husband — the fellow out in the yard — is our crook?"

"Absolutely."

"But ... why on earth —?"

Gloria pointed fiercely at her own temple. "Because like I've been telling you *all afternoon*, the man's not right up in the flippin' loft! He's gone completely and utterly loopy on me. Maybe it's retirement doing it to him, maybe it's just boredom. Either way, justice must be served. It's more than high time he went to jail for his crimes." Through the window Gloria now glared viciously at Quentin, whose latest chore was stacking firewood against the Shelbornes' shed.

Tenderly, Pam said, "You're really sure about all this?"

Gloria turned. "You think I might be *wrong*? You think someone else on the lake just happens to have a pontoon boat that matches my friend's *exact* description?"

"I'm sorry, but —"

"Why don't you rise off your rear end, get out there, and ask him some questions! Some tough, probing questions. See if the old crook doesn't slip up." Gloria folded her arms. "Go on! You'll see!"

Perceiving no option, for Marcy's sake, but to comply, Pam soon stepped outside and approached Quentin. The shed he was stacking firewood against was near shore, and this meant Pam first had to descend a long set of flagstone steps. With negotiating stairs never having been her strongest suit, this gave her plenty of time to think and also to observe. Her 'awakening,' as things went, came in stages.

When only halfway down the steps she could already see that despite Quentin Shelborne being a tall man, his boots were by no means large. By three-quarters down she'd sufficiently thought back to the June weekend Marcy remained in Toronto to work on her reunion. And upon reaching the stairs' bottom landing she spotted the traces of gravel on the pontoon boat's bare wooden deck.

All digested, Pam almost turned at that juncture and began the long ascent back up the stairs. Once again concerned for Marcy's friendship with Gloria, however, she slowly plodded over to Quentin.

After exchanging some quick pleasantries, Pam said to him, "I was wondering — did you happen to lend your pontoon boat to George Clarke back in early June?"

Quentin nodded. "He borrowed it to haul some gravel to your island. Mentioned about working on some paths for Marcy."

"Kind of thought so," Pam said, then put her hands to her face and rubbed tired, closed eyes. When she opened them again she looked up at the cottage, where Gloria and Marcy were standing at the front window. Gloria was jabbing a finger in Quentin's direction.

Turning again to the psychotic vandal, Pam sighed and said, "I'm also betting he used it right till dark, didn't he?"

"Didn't bring it back until about nine, as I recall. Said he really had to hurry to finish even at that hour. Why?"

"Just ... curious," said Pam. Without hesitation now — onlookers be damned — she turned and headed for the stairs.

From behind her she soon heard, "Has Gloria been ranting in there about me refusing to build even more flower beds for her? Is she *still* bloody well going on about that?"

Pam paused in her upward journey, chewed on this latest input a moment, then wearily answered, "No, Quentin, she was actually telling us how wonderful you are."

"I bet."

On her way to her car more than ever now, Pam added, "Just delightfully wonderful."

7

Was the problem hereditary? Her diet? Simply bad luck? Elizabeth Hutton would ponder such issues until her final day. Whatever the cause, from the beginning she worried her daughter was in for a rough ride in life, and those worries proved founded.

Born in 1950 with heart problems and a serious hip deformity, Pam Hutton's childhood in Cambridge was a tiresome and painful blur of doctors' offices and lengthy hospital stays. She underwent the first of several hip operations at age five, desperate attempts to alleviate joint pain and allow greater movement. To some degree these were successful, and at age eight Pam took her first awkward yet unaided steps in this world. But doing so did not mark an end to ailments or pain; her "ticker problems" remained, and what progress she made with walking was limited by concerns over the resulting stress on her heart.

Pam's childhood also proved, for the most part, a lonely childhood. With her parents worrying other offspring might suffer the same ailments, she grew up minus any brothers or sisters. Her health issues also meant she was often away from classmates for weeks or even months at a time. Her father was a sales representative for an industrial equipment manufacturer, and was frequently off on business trips. She did have her mother at home, but despite good intentions, Elizabeth proved a weak substitute for a similar-aged companion.

Pam therefore became accustomed to playing by, and fending for, herself from an early age. But instead of withering, ironically, she grew into quite an independent young lady. She came to stubbornly insist on doing most things for herself, and would have no part of others pitying her. On more than one occasion when she sensed a classmate's visit was parent-provoked, she immediately, out of principle, sent that kid packing. And if ever crossed by anyone, young or old, she invariably displayed she was more than capable of sticking up for herself.

There was the spring, for instance, she spied from her bedroom window several third-grade boys frequently swiping fresh produce from the Huttons' backyard crab apple tree. Pam being again temporarily confined to a wheelchair proved not the least hindrance in her dealing with the matter.

One day, when the boys had once more climbed the tree, she shouted down, "Hey! Do you mind getting the heck out of our apple tree?"

For a moment the boys didn't know where the voice came from. At last, however, they spotted a thin, curly brown-haired girl on a second floor balcony facing the backyard. Studying her wheelchair, one of the boys scoffed and replied, "We'll do whatever we want! What are *you* gonna do about it?"

Several seconds later the first of the crab apples Pam threw bounced off this boy's head. Soon after, he and his partner in crime were nowhere to be seen.

She did, however, also have a softer, gentler side during those early years, one prone to worry and to depression. As she would explain later to a husband, you grow up quickly when ill as a child. Pam was thus still very young when she began understanding her plight in life. Some insights she gleaned from doctors and her own common sense, but the most troubling and thought-provoking usually came from overheard conversations. Pam knew she made a choice to eavesdrop, but often she simply couldn't help herself.

One notable conversation she overheard late on a warm evening in May of 1961, the year she turned eleven. Naturally she was supposed to be in bed, but as often she did, she slipped out on this night to the second-floor balcony. She had discovered in past that voices carried well to this perch. On this particular evening the predicted voices were those of her mother and Aunt Viv — Elizabeth's older sister — who was visiting for a week.

"I was watching her yesterday, moving along as she does," Pam heard her aunt say just after she reached the balcony. "Such a shame for a young girl to grow up so hindered. It seemed the slightest breeze would make her lose her balance."

From Pam's mother came, "She's been through a great deal — more than any child should have to. Things aren't necessarily ever going to get better, either. After sending Pamela to sit in the waiting room, I talked to Dr. Kroft again the other day. He's not certain yet, but he suspects her heart problems are worsening."

"The poor dear. It makes you wonder how things will be for her when she becomes fully grown. What sort of life do you think she'll lead?"

Then came words that would make Pam mostly sleepless on this night, and on many more to come.

Softly, and amid sniffling, her mother replied, "It may seem awful to say, Viv, but the harsh reality is we're not allowing ourselves to look too far ahead with Pamela. We simply can't. We can pray she lives to a hundred, but the fact is, there's a good chance she won't see twenty. It makes me so sad to admit it, but ... we really can't count on her even having a future."

In the summer of 1964 Pam's life took a brighter turn. Well enough to avoid a doctor's office for several weeks she accepted an invitation to stay at a classmate's cottage. Never in her life had she done such a thing, and therefore had no clue what Angie Latrell was drawing her into. At fourteen she was old enough, however, to realize she was long overdue for some adventure.

The girls had a ball together at Green Heron Lake. Angie — red-haired, short, and "plump" — could scarcely have looked much different from her guest, but in personality she was a good match. She had the same devilish sense of humour, and had never been condescending or overly sympathetic concerning her friend's health matters. Her "chocolate éclair problem" also meant Angie was not the most athletic herself, and therefore Pam never felt she was hindering her fun. As a result, each day the girls greatly enjoyed swimming, boating, and generally carrying on. Through all this Pam held up surprisingly well. In fact, one time Elizabeth Hutton called to check on her daughter's health, Pam responded with, "What about it, ma?"

It was on the Monday of the girls' second week that Angie's rather domineering mother, Jackie, insisted the girls join her in visiting a long-time friend. The friend's cottage was on a small island in the lake's eastern section, a twenty minute trip by motorboat.

Nora Ferguson met her visitors at the dock and proceeded to invite them onto her front deck. Pam and Angie found the elderly, ever-smiling lady quite pleasant, but once she and Jackie were deeply embedded in conversation the girls became bored. Nora noticed their yawns soon enough, though, and for the remainder of the afternoon generously granted them the run of the island. This, they noted with glee, despite reservations expressed by Angie's mother.

Initially, like so many others on Green Heron, the girls didn't think much of Whisper Island. But soon enough on this bright, hot day they partook in a swim off the headland, then sunbathed on its broad expanse of granite. Thereafter they began exploring the island's rambling, boulder-strewn shoreline and thickly-wooded interior. For all its aesthetic wants, the girls came to find the island rather exciting, and this primarily for the escape it offered from parental watchings. Indeed, when at last Jackie's call came for the girls to return to the Fergusons' cottage, both did so reluctantly. While lying in bed before sleep the next several evenings they also found themselves recounting at length the unrestricted fun they'd enjoyed on Whisper. Soon enough Angie was even referring to the island as "our little oasis."

What followed was inevitable, although Pam didn't see it coming. By now she was very familiar with Angie's adventurous side, but a proposal her friend delivered the Thursday of that week still caught her by surprise.

Her green eyes almost glowing in the light of the bedroom lamp, Angie said, "I'm telling you — we could climb out the window and go by canoe! My parents sleep like logs after midnight; they'd never hear us."

This sparked a giggling fit in Pam. "You're absolutely crazy, Angie! You *are* kidding me — right?"

She was not kidding.

About 1:00 a.m, after Pam laboriously but successfully crawled out the bedroom window, she joined a patiently waiting Angie. A full moon shone on this night so the girls easily negotiated a quiet route to the dock. They also had little trouble silently rolling over the Latrells' canoe and sliding it into the water. When they had paddled out of hearing range Angie made sure to point out this triumph. Proudly she delivered, "Toldyuh."

The trip took them longer than expected. Several times Pam suggested they turn back, but Angie would have no part of it. "You've got something else on your agenda for tonight, do you?" she once asked. Pam saw little point in replying.

When they at last reached Whisper they went ashore at the headland, and soon enough the two girls began nearly two hours of swimming, mud fights, and rounds of tag. Naturally they aspired to be very quiet, but between involuntary screams, laughter, and splashes they actually made quite a racket. Luckily for the girls the Fergusons had returned to their Whitby home for several days, and so their evening went unhindered.

When they at last ran out of steam they lay on the headland awhile. Their plan was to rest before paddling home. But during this break, gazing up at a clear night sky, they naturally gabbed at length, and without realizing it this only fatigued them further. What happened next Angie later claimed "sort of snuck up on them."

The following morning proved rather eventful. The girls woke early and, in hysterics, soon began frantically paddling home. Not, however, before one Jackie Latrell discovered them missing. What followed was a flurry of telephone calls to neighbouring cottagers and the police beginning a search. Although a passing boater soon spotted the girls in their canoe and immediately delivered them home, the case was far from closed. In addition to several exciting chores, such as painting the cottage's shed, they were given a short leash the remaining three days of their holiday.

During this sentence the girls spent considerable time playing board games inside, and talking, the latter especially after heading to bed. Their room being distant from that of Angie's parents meant they could chat for hours, providing they kept their voices low.

It was on Saturday night, while the girls lay in the dark on their twin beds, that Pam shared something special with Angie.

Angie had just finished 'confessing' to a dream experienced the previous night. She'd been kidnapped by Bryan (a fellow at school with whom Pam was hopelessly in love) and taken to Australia on his sailboat. There he insisted on making her his bride and buying her a hundred dresses, twelve horses, and a huge mansion. "And so we lived happily ever after, Pammy," Angie brazenly ended her account, following which she was half smothered with a pillow.

When Pam was again in her own bed, she said, "Promise you won't laugh if I tell you about a *real* dream?"

"Nope."

"Nope?"

Angie giggled. "Just tell me, you nitwit."

Pam paused a moment, then almost whispering, said, "I had a dream the night we fell asleep on the island."

"Really? Let me guess — you were stranded there with your sweetheart?"

Pam immediately quipped, "Heck no. Somebody in the dream said the bugger ran off with you to Australia."

This prompted another giggling fit from Angie, but soon she mostly recovered and said, "So go ahead, tell me this dream."

After clearing her throat, Pam slowly continued. "Well ... it was of us running around Whisper Island. Doing laps around it, I mean."

"Okay. And?"

Pam raised herself onto an elbow. "You don't understand — we were *running*. Really running. *I* was running."

"You mean as fast as Angie 'The Gazelle' Latrell?"

"Believe it or not, faster. You couldn't even keep up, you poor thing."

"Ha! You *were* dreaming!"

Pam, again softly, said, "I don't know why I had a dream like that, but I do know something."

"What's that?"

"I sure liked it." Pam now smiled warmly, and just enough light came from the hall for a friend to see it.

Springing to her feet, Angie said, "Then we'll have to sneak back, Pammy my girl. We'll have to go back before they drag us home!"

Laughing, Pam waved Angie into bed again. "You're a nutcase! Your mother would stick us in prison this time, or at least make us paint that stupid shed again."

"All worth it."

"Yes, I suppose it would be. But anyway, I do have a question for you."

"Fire away."

Pam once again paused a moment, then said, "Think it's ... sort of dumb? Having a dream like that?"

Lying on her back, Angie had immersed herself in making goofy shadow puppets, but now stopped all silliness and turned to Pam. "Maybe a little. I don't know." Tenderly, she added, "I'm ... not you."

At last resting her head on her pillow, Pam said, "I don't think it's dumb."

The girls returned to Cambridge the following Monday of that summer. With the Latrells soon selling their cottage Pam did not visit Green Heron Lake with Angie again. Upon leaving she did, however, take with her many cherished memories. Especially so her Whisper Island dream, which she even somewhat relived before leaving.

Unable to sleep on her final night, long after hearing Angie's last words Pam slipped from bed and went to the window. There she knelt and rested her folded arms and chin on the sill. On this evening gusts blew, and with each, warm air surged through the screen. And upon closing her eyes, Pam found it easy to imagine herself again running on Whisper — to her came cricket song, the lake's earthy scent, and the feel of summer air rushing through her hair.

Almost four years to the month after that sojourn, Pam's life took another pleasant turn. Indeed, September 3, 1968 brought an event of shocking magnitude. It was one her dazed mother needed three weeks to recover from, and for eighteen-year-old Pam one previously unfathomed: someone actually asked her out.

Roger Marsden had wanted to do so for some time ("or so he said.") Apparently the countless conversations with Pam on collection days years earlier had piqued the paperboy's interest. Now having reached the grand age of twenty-two, and nearing the end of a university engineering program, he evidently had at last mustered the necessary courage — albeit 'phone courage.'

He first received "maybe," of course. This delivered to his ear with a tone suggesting twelve other suitors were on hold at that moment. After a follow-up call, however, Pam did manage to "tuck" Roger in. So it was she launched her first ever date. Roger was to pick her up in his father's car the following Saturday evening.

Despite low expectations — "he was just the paperboy, after all" — that date went well and was soon followed by a string of others. Pam found Roger surprisingly intriguing — a curious blend of simpleton and intellectual, lion and lamb, smooth lady's man and "truckdriver." So intrigued was she, in fact, that she became Pam Marsden less than two years later.

They began their life together living in a Cambridge apartment, but soon bought a house in Toronto. Here Roger had landed a promising position with a large engineering firm. For her part, Pam settled into a secretarial job with an advertising agency, and so the couple soon became comfortable financially. They divided their time between improving their house, entertaining friends, and travelling outside the city on weekends. According to Mrs. Marsden, when their first anniversary arrived all couldn't have been more "peachy."

Pam's health, however, again became problematic. Five months after that first anniversary she once more required surgery on both hips, confining her to a wheelchair for weeks. Half a year later she visited the hospital again — this time for a month — with heart irregularities. "Seems you've married yourself a lemon," Pam croaked to Roger with a weak smile one day. To this he responded by merely fussing over her room, which he merely did the sixteen times a day he visited his lemon.

Luckily, Pam survived that period, and came away more determined than ever to fight her predicament in life. She began studying in depth her particular ailments, spending countless hours in libraries doing research. At this she excelled, and eventually her level of medical knowledge specific to her health problems rivalled that of her doctors. As Roger often joked when she returned from appointments, "So what did they learn from you today?"

Pam also began a strict exercise regime. In addition to stretching with Ed Allen each morning, she insisted on walking over a mile to and from work. This latter component of her daily workout she maintained regardless of weather, prompting Roger to dub her "the mailman." As with her studies, such efforts proved beneficial to her health; she showed marked improvement in her strength, cardiovascular fitness, and flexibility. "Welcome to the new me!" she said one afternoon while modelling a dress Roger bought to congratulate her. His lemon apparently still had a few miles left in her yet.

It was in August of 1973 that she at last allowed her walking routine to be broken for a night. Immediately upon leaving her office and reaching the street she encountered Roger waiting in their shiny blue Pontiac.

"What's up, doc?" she asked through the open passenger window, beaming a puzzled smile.

Roger, still dressed in a silver work suit, said, "Carl in accounting told me last week of a little place we should go for supper. I thought I'd surprise you with it tonight."

After relinquishing her walk, and ensuring someone realized the gesture's gravity, Pam said to the driver, "But you've successfully sparked the old girl's curiosity, hon. So what sort of food are we in for?"

Wearing a sly grin his now storefront-gazing wife didn't notice, Roger answered, "Italian, if I've remembered right."

They were just outside Toronto and heading north on Highway 400 when Pam, previously immersed in work-related conversation, began wondering about their destination. "Where the heck is this place, anyway?" she said to Roger, who with a curious smile answered, "Be patient. Won't be much longer." Yet another hour would pass, though, before he even pulled off the main highway, and then onto what was merely a rural side road.

Pam still didn't have a clue where they were headed when, following several more turns, they reached a lake and tiny dock. But, soon after departing in a boat about which Roger offered only another smile, she most certainly recognized Whisper Island.

Amid sporadic fits of crazed laughter, about four times Pam asked, "What in the heck is going on?!" Roger once again didn't answer; after docking at the Fergusons' he simply led the way to the island's western point. Here, at last, he stopped at an old picnic table. On it sat a large plastic cooler.

"Welcome to 'Fergie's Restaurant,' Roger announced with style, helping Pam onto a seat. "At a general store near here they say Nora makes the best lasagne in the known universe."

Pam needed time on this evening, of course, to digest both her supper and where she now found herself. But when she did she was more than eager to "catch up with an old friend." Together the couple did a full circle of the island, and during this tour, which included a look at George

Clarke's recently-built cabin, Pam talked Roger's ear off. So too Nora Ferguson's, who they encountered late in the walk. Pam complimented the chef's cooking and also her establishment's rustic decor. Sadly, this proved the last time Pam would see Nora, but she left seeing what she saw after her first visit to Whisper — a generous, ever-smiling lady waving from her cottage deck.

It was nearing sunset when they arrived back at the picnic table. Here Roger retrieved the cooler he'd bought in preparation for the evening. Thereafter returning to the Fergusons' spare boat, he took what to Pam seemed a peculiar route. Instead of walking the shore Roger led the way along the edge of the island's woods. Right past, as this route took them, a stake sporting bright orange paint.

This particular round of digestion didn't take Pam long. "Is ... this a *lot* that's been surveyed out?!"

"Yes, it is."

"And is it up for *sale*?"

Somberly, Roger shook his head and answered, "No, I'm afraid it isn't." That head soon stopped shaking, however, and with his grimace transforming into a mischievous grin, he added, "Not any more."

They built the following spring. And as Roger frequently teased, when on Whisper that first magical season Pam's feet hardly touched the ground. Between the island itself and those she would share it with, Pam didn't know where to begin in thanking Roger. Nor, as it went, the other source of this godsend.

Following their picnic the previous year she naturally inquired into the details of their new acquisition. Seemed an old friend, one that had married and moved west, remembered a certain conversation from years earlier. When that old friend received news through her mother the Fergusons were selling, she was not long in sending a letter to Roger's office. "Angie 'The Gazelle' Latrell — you are my hero!" was how Pam reacted to this revelation.

In years following the Marsdens would blend well with their fellow islanders. However, as usual desiring no sympathies, Pam shared little of her life-long ailments with others on Whisper. What the community gleaned of her past they did so from Roger and Pam's parents, who visited once a year. But when Pam again had to undergo surgery in the spring of 1989 her fellow islanders allowed themselves a certain "nosiness" and proceeded to help the couple as much as possible. Evan kept their lawn mowed, basement tenant Marcy did all their cooking in Toronto, and when Roger ventured north alone for a break, George always took him fishing. To this day, mention of either these gestures, or countless others in years following, leave Pam Marsden teary-eyed.

As for her childhood dream on Whisper, Pam unfortunately did not have a reoccurrence. "That would have been the Cinderella ending, but I'll live," she said to Roger as they lay in bed one evening. Yet occasionally, and unbeknownst to Roger, just after dawn she slips from bed and ventures along Whisper's shore, her favourite stretch being that near the very musical Finch Cove. What she sometimes does during those outings she considers goofy, but does anyway. After psyching herself up she breaks into an awkward jog, followed soon by total collapse, but also a familiar girlish giggle. And during that short run a dream is indeed relived — even if just for a moment.

8

On the Friday preceding 2002's August long weekend Pam Marsden arrived at Whisper much later than usual. On this day Roger became "hopelessly hog-tied" at work and, upon hours passing, urged Pam by phone to journey lakeward ahead of him. Being on her own for an evening did not particularly bother her, mind you; she cherished occasional time alone at the lake. Her only grievance was losing precious hours to the city. When she finally arrived at the island nine o'clock arrived with her, and light was fading.

During a quick stop at Kirkdale's she learned the lake's week had been hot and rainless. So, even after transferring groceries and other weekend paraphernalia from boat to cottage — a task for her always especially awkward and tiring — she stubbornly set about watering her flowers. These she maintained in stylish cedar planters scattered across the property.

She began with those nearest her shed's lakeside wall, on which hung her garden hose reel. She then progressively moved to planters father away, and in so doing drew out more and more hose. The most distant of her flowers were difficult to attend to because the hose didn't reach; she'd never got around to buying another section. Rather than going to the "enormous palaver" of filling a watering jug, however, she simply turned the nozzle to 'stream' and doused the remaining plants from a distance. This in combination with stretching the hose absolutely as far as it would go.

The Marsdens' shed, built prior to the cottage, had unquestionably seen better days. Rotted and splintered, Roger had a new shed on his list of 'must-dos' for the summer of 2002 (the fifth consecutive year the project enjoyed this status.) The Marsdens joked but so decrepit was the tiny building that its contents were truly all that kept it standing.

When drawing the garden hose to its maximum reach that Friday evening, and exerting pressure on the reel, Pam never gave a thought to the shed. What she didn't yet realize was its padlock was smashed, and the building's entire contents — meaning its critical supports — were presently floating on the lake's surface or resting on its bottom. Consequently, when she stretched the garden hose the shed proceeded to collapse. Worse, she had hardly comprehended this sudden catastrophe when another struck she was not witness to.

The lakeside wall of the Marsdens' shed not only impressively supported a garden hose reel but also one end of a clothesline. Since two supports are the norm for such, when the shed fell over it naturally did its own pulling, and what it pulled on — fiercely — was an equally aged flagpole.

And consumed with staring dazedly at the collapsed shed, Pam didn't even see the slender thirty-foot pole coming.

Roger Marsden prided himself on being a law-abiding citizen, especially concerning driving. "If we all head north like maniacs every weekend, some will miss the festivities — for good," he often lectured. But if it must be known, that first August Friday in 2002 his tires pretty much left a trail of flames.

When he reached the tiny hospital in Birchport he found the entire island crew already present. Pam was woozy but nonetheless conscious, and when Roger entered her room he found her even cracking jokes.

"Roger?" she croaked, pawing at the air. "Roger, is ... that ... you? Roger?"

"Bloody hilarious!" the husband countered harshly. That delivered he proceeded to smother further antics with a lengthy hug, followed by assorted fussings over Pam's bed and room trappings. At this he was obviously no novice.

Once finished these chores Roger turned to George. "Now — what the heck happened?"

"Nothing more to report than what I said on the phone," George answered. "I was whistling over to your place to visit my sweetie here when I found her having a nap. Thought it was strange she'd have one under a flag pole but hey, to each their own."

Roger said to Pam, "Any idea how long you were unconscious?"

"Not exactly. I arrived at the lake about nine, and George says he found me about twenty after. Allowing for my work in between I'd say five minutes maybe — that's all."

"That's all, she says," Roger offered sarcastically to a seated Evan. He then turned away from the group and let go a vicious round of cursing under his breath. When he turned back spit lingered on his lower lip. "I'll spill blood for this."

Pam quickly said, "That is not the answer, honey. Yes, I

got hurt — a little glancing blow to the noggin — but if you go off to battle we'll just end up with —"

"One thing to be a vandal, another to be a murderer!" Roger cut in. "You call it a little glancing blow if you want, but you easily could have been killed. Don't deny it."

George said, "Not to excuse whoever did the number on the shed but I really don't think they intended anyone physical harm, Rog. They couldn't have seen what emptying that shed would amount to."

"Emptying our shed?"

George now realized he hadn't offered this tidbit over the phone. Sighing, he said, "'Fraid most of your items are mingling with the fish right now. The rest floated away, it seems. Dorothy Burke over on the mainland already called me wondering about a wicker chair."

As Roger began another round of barely-concealed cursing, Marcy piped in, "Was she looking to buy a new one, George?"

Her soul mate only stared at her vacantly a second, then moved to the hall, where Roger had retired to finish his tantrum. There he soothingly said, "I'd say the stuff that sunk we can fish out — it's not that deep off your place."

"Oh, I'm aware," Roger answered wearily. "It's not losing all our junk or the shed that's bothering me, though, and you know it. It's the bloody *nerve* of this moron, and the fact I've got a wife in there who's already spent half her life in the hospital. Believe me, she doesn't need this."

From inside Pam's room came Marcy's cheery voice. "I was looking at new wicker chairs just last week. They've got some lovely ones here in the village at Davison's."

"Yes, I realize, Rog," George continued. "I also agree something has to be done; this is the capper. Now that Pam's at least settled we'll get on the phone to the police and file a hefty report."

Roger waved a finger in dissent. "No. Actually, I've got another idea in mind, now that I've calmed down a bit. I don't want you telling anyone on the lake this incident even happened. In a minute I'll be asking our fellow islanders to do the same."

George offered a puzzled expression. "What've you got in mind?"

"Self-justice," Roger quickly answered, brashly. Then in a more reserved tone he said, "You'll see."

Pam left the hospital on Monday of the long weekend and even returned to work on Wednesday of that week. "So, all in all, no harm done," she contended at supper in Toronto after that first day of work. This she did in a desperate but fruitless attempt to quell an inevitable storm; one look at her husband told her trouble was brewing.

That trouble surfaced just over a week later, on the middle Friday of August. Evan had no sooner arrived at the island than Roger was dragging him over to the Marsden cottage. George, Evan soon learned, had already received the same treatment.

With the lads beveraged and settled at the Marsdens' picnic table Roger wasted no further time.

"I've set a trap," he delivered the second his posterior hit the seat.

George just as quickly eyed him quizzically. "You've set a *what*?"

"I put the word out around the lake you two were taking

off fishing for the weekend. I bragged it up pretty good; told a few chatty types you had yourselves a peach of a mudhole north of here. And I really do think they bought it."

"But ... how's that a trap, Roger?" Evan innocently asked.

With a sigh came, "It's a trap, Mr. Dean, because whoever's doing all this stuff will learn of your little trip and see a prime opportunity. I'm betting dollars to donuts this idiot'll be around tomorrow night in the wee hours." Roger grinned slyly, almost a touch psychotically it seemed to George. "Of course, we'll be waitin' to welcome him, boys."

George chewed on this a minute, then asked. "How do we know whose place he'll hit?"

Roger shrugged. "He's already done a few numbers on yours. The Deans' he hasn't even touched yet. Not that we know of, at least."

"Where exactly are we going to hole up during this little stakeout? We're fine for visibility out the front of Evan's place, but I'm not so sure about the back."

"I've already figured that out too," Roger answered matter-of-factly. "We won't hide in the cottage; we'll sit in Evan's old tree house."

"She's up to the task," the owner added proudly.

Roger, eyebrows innocently high after this reassuring remark, stared at George. "I assume, then, Evan's in. What I need to know right now is — are *you* with me? Because if you are, we'll have to keep both of you out of sight after tonight; I put the word out you'd be taking off early tomorrow morning. You both will have to stay inside our place for the day."

George breathed deeply, looked out to the lake, then nodded. "I don't imagine weekends will be much fun anyway till we clear this mess up."

Roger turned to Evan. "And you'll keep your head

screwed on straight?" He eyeballed the island's youngest resident.

"Of course, Rog," Evan answered. Then, even more defensively, he shifted awkwardly in his seat and again offered, "Of course."

9

Like George Clarke and the Marsdens, young John and Emily Dean were drawn to Whisper when the Fergusons put the island up for sale. In contrast to the others, however, the Deans were lured merely by the Fergusons' real estate listing, and they considered the island property only one possibility among many. Initially they also were not overly impressed. The shoreline of the island's last remaining lot seemed too shallow and boulder-strewn, and, as budding naturalists, they feared too many trees would require felling to accommodate a cottage. Indeed the couple were about to cross off this particular listing and continue their search when something happened to change their minds.

John Dean hadn't thought cottage lot hunting on that September Saturday of 1973 a "super idea," but Emily insisted her due date was still distant enough; they were hardly at the eight month mark, for goodness sake. But perhaps she was underestimating, as John later suggested, "the nature of the beast." For on a patch of spruce-sheltered bedrock late that sunny afternoon, Emily Dean would ultimately give birth to a bouncing five-pound-eight-ounce boy.

The new family's future concerning Whisper now seemed unavoidable: how, after all, could you dismiss the very earth upon which your dear child was born? For all its seeming wants, the last lot on Whisper now just had to be theirs.

The couple built a modest cottage the following spring — the same season the Marsdens built — choosing a thin L-shaped design that kept tree destruction to a minimum. In time they did come to look at their lot, and the island in general, in a positive light. Emily enjoyed wandering the lake paths during early evening, while a more athletic John found pleasure in swimming off the headland. The couple also gelled nicely with the island's other residents.

For young Evan, once he gained his legs the island and lake became a world of wondrous curiosities, and his parents had to watch him closely, so inclined was he to wander. His neighbours gave him full run of Whisper and he made good use of the privilege. This they only did until Evan reached about the age of seven, however, because it was then "things turned a corner." The 'nature of the beast' to which John Dean long referred now came to light.

Evan's first major setback occurred on a weekend in late June of 1986, the year he turned thirteen. On Saturday night — three days prior to Canada Day — John Dean intended to treat fellow islanders and a dozen mainlanders to a fireworks display. These he would ignite on 'Evan Isle,' a tiny, barren-rock islet some fifty yards off the Deans' shore. This with enthusiastic spectators seated in lawn chairs in front of the Deans' cottage. Having looked forward to the event for some time, John hoped for "a sparkler of an evening."

Ironically, a sparkler is exactly what brought about his plan's demise. Near dusk, after John had loaded a crate of fireworks into his boat and was about to depart for the launch site, Evan decided his help would be needed. He also judged that taking along his burning sparkler would make for a stunning visual effect as they cruised to the islet.

It was about a second after John noticed his son in the

boat, still tied to the dock, that the first firework went off. That one luckily soared straight into the sky and burst, as advertised, into a flower of bright red stars. But the second firework, and many of those following, proceeded to launch at angles decidedly closer to horizontal. One, in fact, narrowly missed the nearby head of George Clarke, who avoided the impact by jumping off the dock into the lake. Another zigzagged into the row of lawn chairs, while yet another — a roman candle — soared through the Dean's kitchen window. And so on. By the time the last firework ignited no one was within a hundred yards of the Deans' boat, and several hours passed before Emily managed to sip coffee unaided. So ended Canada Day celebrations for 1986.

Unfortunately, this proved only the beginning of Evan's "accidents." In years following he would chalk up countless others, and predictably develop a reputation on Green Heron as a disaster waiting to happen.

Among the most notable was the mishap of 1989, the year Evan successfully reached sixteen. That summer he landed himself a job at a bakery working a night owl shift from closing time at 6:00 p.m until 2:00 a.m. Normally, preceding his days off he would return home after his last shift to sleep before heading to Whisper. But one evening in early July he decided he would travel north immediately after work. He knew how to sneak into the cottage without waking his parents; in the morning he would therefore be a major surprise.

He arrived at Ferg Landing about 4:00 a.m, and naturally it was still dark. This, Evan would later contend, was the "main factor" in what transpired.

Although he had by now made numerous trips to the island on his own, including in the dark, this time he somehow became a touch disoriented. From the landing you approach Whisper from the southwest and first encounter, head-on, two points: the Marsdens' to your left and Marcy's to your right. To reach the Dean cottage you must curl around Marcy's point and continue along the island's east shore. Quite straightforward, but for some reason, on the morning in question Evan forgot about Marcy's point. And in the dark— and at full speed, of course — the shore "came out of nowhere." By the time the boat stopped it was twenty-five feet onto that shore — meaning Marcy Willett's front lawn — and had demolished (in order) a canoe, three wooden planter boxes, an antique birdbath, a patio table, and two ceramic gnomes.

Evan remained seated after this performance for some fifteen minutes, so stunned and puzzled was he over what exactly went wrong. Eventually, however, he concluded "what was done, was done," and, with no sign of Marcy waking, moped his way home. Yes, his parents were in for a major surprise, all right.

To cap things off for poor Evan, not only did his summer's pay go toward replacing Marcy's ruined property, to this day he has yet to regain his boat. Later that morning, after breaking the bad news to his parents, Evan and John journeyed to inspect the damage and remove the boat. They feared Marcy would be in great distress, but when they arrived they found her in unusually good spirits. Not only was she not concerned about her damaged property (in fact she seemed oblivious to it), she was quietly singing to herself, planting "the loveliest marigolds" in a curious new planter already half filled with soil.

But, by all accounts, Evan's finest moment undoubtedly came five years later — in February of 1994 — when he visited Whisper on his own for a weekend.

He arrived at Green Heron from Orangeville about 10:00 a.m. on Saturday. Immediately he was thrilled with how much snow the area had received (he loved lots of snow), and also with the fellow cottagers he bumped into at Kirkdale's. Along with several male friends, a trio of "chickarooskies" had also ventured north with their parents. So began what proved an eventful weekend.

The group of six snowmobiled trails most of Saturday. Evan and one of the girls rode on George Clarke's ancient machine, which was stored in his cargo trailer at Ferg Landing. Luckily Evan managed to get through the day without damaging it, and feeling he should celebrate this tremendous feat, his friends coaxed him into hosting a party that evening.

That event was rather lively. Since no cottagers close by were up, the group of six could be as loud and crazy as they pleased. At one point, in his inebriated stupor, Evan didn't know which to worry about more — a woodstove that was almost glowing it was so hot, or his two buddies playing football near the large front windows. His luck won out again, however, and he awoke in his bedroom the next morning (an achievement in itself, he considered) to not only a cottage that was fine but also his "babe of choice" warmly nestled at his side. More, when he stumbled out to the living room he was greeted by a picturesque view — large, fluffy snowflakes slowly descending over the lake and front deck. In the end, a finer weekend Evan could not have fathomed, and he soon drove home whistling.

It was in mid-April of that year, right after the ice went out on Green Heron, that John Dean made a trip north to open up the cottage. It was also then he discovered that cottage half collapsed.

"Let me get this straight," he soon inquired by phone

from Kirkdale's. "I sent you up here in February to shovel the snow off the roof. I hope you're not about to tell me ... "

Silence on the other end, then a sigh.

Following years of such incidents, John and Emily were at a loss how to help Evan. Countless times they talked with him at length, but all such chats resulted in little progress.

During Thanksgiving weekend of 1994, soon after the Deans put the finishing touches on their newly-rebuilt cottage, John and Emily discussed the matter in private in their screened sitting room.

"Perhaps he'll simply grow out of it," John suggested, wishfully.

"Sure," said Emily, "But will he live that long? Will *we* live that long?"

"I think figuring out the root of his problem is important. George Clarke claims Evan "gets sidetracked a lot," whatever that means."

Emily said, "I think I know. He means Evan always seems to have good intentions behind what end up as accidents and screw-ups; he's invariably out to please people. It's simply that he's *so* determined to please he gets careless."

John grinned. "That's a wonderfully positive spin on the matter."

"Go ahead and scoff. I fully believe in what I say. It's not merely a mother sticking up for her son."

"Okay."

Emily sighed. "Regardless, this is obviously an issue that will soon come to a head. Certain promises *will* be kept, my love, and that means a torch will need to be passed."

"I'm aware," said John, wearily. "But I think we both know what will then happen."

"We do?"

John smartly answered, "Sure. Evan'll be so out to please his old lady he'll drop the torch and burn the place down. The good part is — that'll actually simplify things."

Another sigh, then, "You're entirely heartless, Mr. Dean."

The promise Emily Dean referred to was one made by John before the two even married. Upon retirement they would move to Emily's childhood hometown of Sydney, Nova Scotia. This in trade for their living up to this time in John's Ontario hometown of Orangeville. The 'passing of the torch' they referred to was naturally guardianship (if not ownership) of the cottage on Whisper. Evan could retain the cottage, or his parents could sell.

John and Emily, both school teachers, had also planned well ahead for early retirement; they would do so while only in their mid-fifties. Specifically, they would end their working careers in 1997, and therefore it was then that Evan needed to make a decision: stay or go.

"Stay!" he immediately declared in June of that year.

John said, "Then here's the deal. We'll give you three years to show us you can keep this cottage alive and well. If you do, you'll get it as an early inheritance. If you mess up, though, we'll be selling the place, Evan.

"We care about the neighbours," Emily added, "and it's simply not fair to have them constantly living in fear either of you or for you. Do you understand all this?"

"I understand."

So, following a farewell party for the Deans, Evan

assumed control over the family cottage. And naturally his fellow islanders began worrying. They truly did want Evan to succeed, even if the likes of George or Roger would never admit it. All therefore made efforts to keep Evan out of trouble, and all collectively held their breath.

One pastime George often encouraged in Evan was fishing. He figured if the young Dean was at least within his view he could help keep him out of trouble. This also suited Evan fine; he'd long enjoyed spending time alone with George. Less 'heady' than Pam or Roger, he found the older islander easy to open up to.

"I just get so *worried*," he said to George one evening in the boat while untangling his line for the fifth time. "I know it'll only take one big screwup — maybe even a little one — and I'll be toast."

George paused from his own brand of fishing, in which a lure actually got put in the water. "Open to suggestions, Mr. Dean."

"Heck yes."

"The next time you get one of your … *ideas* … about helping someone or pleasing them?"

"Okay?"

"First sit on it an hour or two."

"Think it all through first, you mean?"

"No, I mean … pull up a chair on your deck or lawn, and just sit there."

"And do what?"

"Nothing!"

Evan naturally assumed George was merely teasing him, and therefore initially resented his words. For several weeks he refused to go fishing, and pretty much gave his other neighbours the cold shoulder as well.

But then one day, after several friends suggested he

throw a doozy of a party — since he no longer cared about his neighbours — Evan wound up taking George's advice. He did so somewhat by accident, ironically. During a windy morning a branch had broken off a maple and landed on his cottage's roof. Upon descending a ladder after removing the debris, Evan slipped, fell to the ground, and slightly sprained his wrist while rolling. Thereafter he lay in a lounge chair, stewing over his bad luck.

Eventually he fell asleep and by the time he woke it was late afternoon. Luckily he had placed the lounge chair in deep shade, and so he was not sunburnt. In fact, he felt quite refreshed, and remained in the chair another hour.

Doing, as George suggested, absolutely nothing.

When at last rising, he immediately phoned his friends and informed them there would be no party. If they had already foolishly spread word, those party-goers were in for a disappointment.

So Evan continued over the remainder of that summer, and also over the next two. As silly or even crazy as it seemed, whenever he developed the inkling to help, please, or otherwise impress someone, he first made himself sit in his lounge chair at least a half hour. Sometimes he still ultimately proceeded with his original plan, but not once did it result in disaster.

He soon learned, however, that it was not only George helping him. First, whenever other neighbours noticed him in his lounge chair, they backtracked home. But the island, curiously, also played a role. For some reason, up until he began his newfound habit he'd never really stopped and *listened* to Whisper Island; his visual experience had always dominated. Now, though, laying motionless with his eyes closed, he heard the lake lapping against the shore, breezes through the trees above him, insects buzzing around him, and in the distance, the calls of birds. Together he found these sounds soothing, and helpful in his doing 'nothing.'

"Somehow you and that island have slowed down his whole world," John Dean commented to George on the phone one night from Sydney.

"You'd never thought of it?" George asked.

"Sure we'd *thought* of it, but it's illegal to tie your kid up, isn't it?"

In the end, Evan got through his three years of 'probation.' Indeed, when his parents visited Whisper the summer of 1999 they claimed the family cottage looked in better shape than it ever had. Evan's fellow islanders also vouched that his record was clean. The net result — which Evan awaited with all fingers and toes crossed — was a promise being fulfilled.

That very evening, before they returned to Nova Scotia, John and Emily granted Evan his early inheritance. The cottage on Whisper was his.

The 'handover' was cause for a party, of course. This the islanders threw for Evan on a Friday night in September. Pam and Roger provided the food, George the beverages, and Marcy her cheerful self. The event passed with traditional Whispertonian revelry and Evan was unquestionably the most keen participant. Always, though, he displayed his keenness under the watchful eyes of his neighbours.

As George and Evan sat fishing together near the Charity Isles the following evening, Evan, now "pumped," treated himself to some future-minded speculation.

"It's only a matter of time before I find the apple of my eye," he said, successfully casting his lure to the edge of some pickerelweeds. "Then maybe we'll end up with some of our own little Evans — or little Susies or whatever — running around the island. Just a matter of time, I'd say."

"Uh-huh," said George, trembling (shuddering) at the thought.

"Who knows," Evan continued dreaming aloud, "we might even need to build a second cottage one day."

"There's sure tons of room over on your side of the island." George added stress to that last handful of words.

"In the meantime, it's sure nice to have the ol' monkey off the back." After another cast, Evan turned to George. "I really had something to prove to my parents, you know."

"I know you did, and you won, Ev. We're all real proud of you, and I mean that."

Evan beamed a smile toward Whisper, where several mergansers swam smoothly near shore. "I'm a full-fledged member of the family now, not just the kid of one. Heck ... maybe we should light off some fireworks or something."

"No, no!" George said quickly and firmly, gaining a detailed image in his head. "Maybe don't do that. Just soak up the victory, bud. Trust me — just lay in the ol' lounger and soak'er up."

10

Roger and his two recruits climbed into the Dean tree house about ten o'clock on their planned Saturday evening, not long after darkness fell upon Whisper. In doing so they were careful; the region was at last blessed with rain and the house's tall wooden access ladder was slippery. They would need to keep this circumstance in mind, Roger noted, when descending to "nab our boy," an event he fully expected.

Once seated comfortably in lawn chairs Roger and George, making their first visit to Evan's treasured childhood retreat, apparently couldn't help considering its builder. Frequently during the evening both would scan the house — which amounted to a tiny, crooked, and sparsely-clad cabin wedged among three maples — and nervously study every rusty nail and weathered plank. Evan, occasionally noticing these inspections, could only counter with, "*What*?"

But on the positive side, at an altitude of twenty feet Evan's tree house offered a fine and secretive view of the Dean cottage. This available through several tiny glassless windows the men huddled near. Also, following the rain the sky had cleared and a three-quarter moon now shone, making visibility excellent.

For the first several hours they watched diligently.

Beyond that, however, with no signs of anyone, their effort became increasingly lax. Optimism was waning; perhaps no one would come after all, perhaps their vandal had somehow been tipped off. As such, spirits descended, yawn rates rose, and the end result was predictable: by 3:00 a.m both George and Evan had dozed off, leaving only Roger on watch.

It was about 4:30 a.m when the sleepers were nudged awake by the watchman's boot. With an index finger to his lips to signal both to keep silent, Roger pointed with his other toward the Deans' cottage.

George, who had migrated from his chair to the tree house's floor during his sleep, rose to his knees and crept to the front window. After rubbing cobwebs from his eyes he scanned the moonlit lot. Initially he neither saw nor heard anything. Whispering, he said to Roger, "Are you sure?"

George didn't need an answer, because right then came a creaking sound, one he quickly recognized as that made by a loose deck plank. Peering out again, this time in the direction of the Deans' side door, George saw a tall figure apparently in the midst of picking the lock. At his feet were a crow bar and small tool kit.

"The eagle has landed, boys," Roger whispered. "We'll let the idiot inside so we'll at least have break-and-enter on him, then we'll go introduce ourselves."

Within a minute the cottage door was open and the figure disappeared inside, closing the door again behind him. Seconds after, with Roger leading the way, the three men started down the tree house ladder. It had dried somewhat by this time and all descended without incident.

Slowly they crept toward the cottage. The tree house was merely some thirty yards from the side door, but with the critical necessity of remaining quiet they restricted themselves to a very slow pace. By 'they' is implied George and Roger only, however, because with a vandalizing stranger now in his family's cottage Evan was not so disciplined. Indeed, soon after leaving the ladder he stumbled into a retired propane barbecue, hard enough to knock the cast iron lid onto the surrounding bedrock.

The resulting racket, which Roger would later describe as "three drunken brass bands colliding," was more than enough to alert the burglar of the evening. With almost the same racket he burst back out the Deans' side door and sprinted for the dock. He moved incredibly swiftly, and within seconds he'd untied an open aluminium boat, had the outboard running, and was away.

Such a speedy exit the three islanders had not bargained for, but they soon enough agreed on an emergency plan. Racing southwest along one of the island's interior paths the three men jumped into Roger's bowrider, and in less than a minute they too were away. During such, however, they noticed a handful of lights come on at various points on the mainland. "Super!" Roger growled. "We've got the whole bloody lake bothered now." Annoyed even more he immediately jammed the boat to full throttle.

Luckily they soon spotted the fleeing boat. Not only did the evening's three-quarter moon make its aluminium shine, but its outboard was noisy. "He sure enough didn't come into Evan's dock under power with that thing," Roger said to George. "Must have shut it down real early and rowed in." But noisy as the outboard was, it also evidently was running well because Roger only barely kept pace.

A four kilometer finger of land named Camlen Point essentially divides Green Heron into two sections, or what cottagers commonly call wings in light of the lake's butterfly shape. Whisper lies roughly in the centre of the eastern wing, and to the north is a seemingly endless maze of bays and islands large and small. Green Heron is a lake, therefore, on which a boater can easily become lost, especially at night.

And also especially if one so desires.

Such was what Roger, George, and Evan were up against as they cruised north at full tilt. While Roger kept his eyes on the water immediately ahead, George and Evan maintained theirs on the target, which was a quarter of a mile distant. The islanders worried that if the individual at the helm knew the lake well he could easily disappear.

As things went, this is exactly what happened. In seemingly an instant George and Evan both lost sight of the aluminium boat. "Where the heck did he go?" they clamoured in unison, desperately scanning the moonlit lake.

When reaching the spot they last saw the boat, Roger brought his own to a full stop and killed the motor so they could listen. This they did nearly a minute but heard nothing, and all feared the worst.

But then came a familiar drone slightly to the east, and gradually it grew louder. Just about the time George spotted the boat and shouted "There!" it all but ran into them. Fortunately the driver managed to turn at the last second and avoid a collision. Not, however, before soaking the islanders. Motivated even more, immediately Roger fired up his boat again and resumed chase.

"Either he doesn't know the lake or he's none too bright," Roger said with a smug glance at George, who nodded; by now they surmised their fugitive had pulled into Mackley Inlet, which offered no exit. With his apparent mistake the gap between him and the islanders essentially dissolved. Roger's boat was now less than a hundred yards behind.

Just before reaching the northern tip of Green Heron's eastern wing the aluminium boat made a sharp turn to the east and zipped through what was known as Holland Narrows. In following, Roger had to cautiously heed the lake markers; more than one boat had been wrecked here and more than one life lost. "Careful, careful," George reminded him.

Once through the narrows and headed south, a variety of options lay available for the fleeing vandal. But by this time George had a notion, and when the boat ahead of him soon turned east again his suspicions were reinforced.

What they now entered was half marsh and entirely devoid of cottages. George already knew from daytime fishing visits the far end of Davis Bay had become virtually impenetrable by motorboat, so rich had its shallow waters become with cattails, pickerelweed and water lilies. He therefore soon told Roger to stop the boat. "Trim her right up and just let her drift to the shore beside us, Rog. We're gonna have to hoof it from here."

Their 'friend', meanwhile, had continued on and into the marsh by rowing, and although George suspected even this would be difficult, he seemed to make decent progress. Indeed, soon enough the islanders caught a flash of metal in the moonlight indicating he had made it through to the bay's far eastern shore.

"The bugger's probably home free now," Roger snarled in disgust as he tried negotiating the spongy soil along the islanders' portion of southern shore, which in the dark proved almost impossible. As Evan was about to switch on his flashlight — an aid they had wanted to avoid since it would reveal their whereabouts — George grabbed his hand. "No, no. Don't worry, boys. I know where this guy's headed now, and I also know a good way to get there."

Without further explanation, and motioning to his partners to stay quiet and follow, George journeyed up the shore and away from the marsh. He moved surprisingly quickly in the bush, Roger and Evan had always found, and forever being whipped by branches and tripped by rocks the two were pressed to keep up. They eventually received some help, however, because after about five minutes of hiking George came to a halt. When Roger and Evan reached him he pointed along a narrow channel before them that snaked through the woods. "Snowmobile trail."

The going was considerably easier now and the men made much better headway. They were also able to move more quietly, which to George seemed a critical necessity. Occasionally he would order a complete halt and have all train their ears on the trail ahead. Other than faint and typical forest rustlings, however, they heard nothing.

They continued this pattern of stop-listen-go the next ten minutes. To Roger and Evan the trail appeared to be leading nowhere, prompting both to quietly and politely question George's plan, but then all at once they came upon a small clearing. And there, near its far edge, sat a tiny cabin.

"What's this?" Roger asked the pathfinder in a light whisper.

"An old hunting cabin. I used to stop here on occasion back in my snowmobiling days." Pointing a thumb at the small building, George added, "And apparently I'm not the only one familiar with it."

After Roger quickly suggested to Evan they avoid repeating an earlier fiasco, the three men slowly and quietly crept toward the cabin. Once at the door, which was closed, Roger nudged George to get his attention, then counted to three with his fingers. On what would have been four they together kicked the door and promptly removed it from its hinges.

Dramatic and sudden as this entrance may have been, a flashlight soon revealed it surprised no one: save for a wooden table and chairs and a busted, mouse-infested cot the cabin was empty. "Damn it," Roger snapped, kicking over one of the chairs. Thereafter he began searching the cabin for at least signs their man had been inside, but even this yielded nothing.

So too did a search outside, which they conducted several minutes later in what was now a dawn-lit clearing. They were hoping to find tracks leading away, enabling them to continue pursuit, but this effort also proved to no avail. Seemingly they were snookered.

It was at this moment, though, Evan pointed to something dawn did reveal. Nestled among alders behind the cabin, and looking equally as aged, was an outhouse.

Roger turned to George. "Do you think?!"

"I'd say very low odds, but what the hell," came the reply, and so the three men approached the tiny building.

"Naw," Roger grumbled after opening the door to nothing but a cracked toilet seat. However, as he turned to continue searching elsewhere Evan pursued what George considered a long shot nothing shy of ridiculous: he lifted the lid. It was then George was forced to realign his thinking. "You have absolutcly got to be kidding me," he whispered.

There, peering up at them in the soft early light, was a fearful, muck-covered face. And, just so happens, one quite familiar.

11

"But could you just loosen 'em a *little*?" came the plea for a sixth time. "I ain't goin' nowhere, Rog. Honest."

Arnold Knapp — Kirkdale's long-time, trusty mechanic — was currently tightly fastened with boat tie lines to a wooden chair in the hunting cabin. "Arnie ol' boy," as he had recently been dubbed, hadn't struggled at all since the three islanders pushed over the outhouse and dragged him out of the pit. Once his identity was known he immediately seemed to accept defeat. But to add emphasis to the severity of the moment, and clearly a dose of fear, Roger decided on the ropes.

That particular islander was now pacing back and forth in front of Arnold sporting an extremely grave face, one well lighted by morning sun streaming through the cabin's lone window. Arnold's forehead shone with sweat, and out of further nervousness he occasionally rubbed his boots together. This drew the islanders' attention to not only bits of toilet paper still clinging to them but also their dimensions. How curious, George considered, that in all the years he'd known Arnold he'd never noticed his size fourteens. He might have drawn a connection between the mechanic and the boot prints he discovered earlier in the summer. Then again — would he? Good old *Arnold* responsible for all the vandalism? As George sat in his own chair he struggled to wrap his head around it.

Ignoring the prisoner's plea, Roger, detective-like, continued with, "So let's take it from the top. You say Reed Ferguson — Gord and Nora's upstanding son, and Marcy's oh so wonderful cousin — hired you in the spring of 2000? You've been vandalizing us *that* long?"

Arnold nodded. "I'm really sorry, guys. I've been struggling bad, and the money —"

"Yes, you've kindly mentioned the cash a few times now. But anyway, what exactly did Reed say he had in mind?"

"He didn't. I told you, Rog — he didn't tell me why he wanted me to do all this stuff, and I didn' ask. I suppose he wants to get rid of you folks, but I don't know why."

"You're sure about that answer."

Arnold swallowed nervously. "I'm sure. Honest."

"Honest?!" Roger said with a laugh. "At this point, why should I trust a single bloody word you say?"

Arnold sighed. "I wasn' out to hurt you guys. There was nothin' personal about it. I just ... *needed the mon—*"

"Not out to hurt us?! My other half, for one, ended up in the hospital! You call that not hurting us?"

Arnold stared at him quizzically. "She got hurt?" This prompted a quick explanation from Evan, to which Arnold responded with, "Didn' figure on nothin' like that. I'm real sor—"

"You're very sorry. Yes, I know," Roger finished for him. "You just needed the money real bad. Yeah, you mentioned all that." In frustration Roger dragged his fingers through what had become very dishevelled hair.

George now said, "I'm curious about something — whose place did you do a number on first back in that spring of 2000?"

Arnold offered, "Can't really remember now, George. Somebody or other."

Roger kicked the chair — hard. "I'm sorry? You can't —?"

He broke off, because right before delivering a second kick Arnold quietly said, "Buried garbage under George's side porch. It was Reed's idea; thought it might draw over a bear or two from the mainland."

George, who had been sitting relatively calmly next to a standing Evan, now curled his fingers into fists. He only managed to rise from his chair, however, when Evan and Roger intercepted him. "I almost got my ass torn off!" he roared while being restrained.

"I'm a ton sorry for that one, George."

"You're *gonna* be a ton sorry!"

Arnold received yet more nasty threats from George, but luckily Roger and Evan eventually managed to get him seated again.

"You're a special sort of guy, Arnie ol' boy," Roger said, shaking his head. "But that compliment delivered, the next thing I want to know is when you last talked to your buddy Reed?"

"Back in the spring. He dropped in at the garage."

"And?"

"And he gave me some more cash and told me to go ..."

"Yes?"

A moment's pause, then, "To go a little harder this summer. Said he wanted more pressure on you folks. He also said to keep doin' stuff only on weekends. That way you'd less likely consider locals like me, and you'd be more scared and ticked off since stuff was bein' done right in your faces."

"So you said, 'Sure, no problem'?"

To this Arnold only shrugged.

Evan piped in with, "Didn't Reed worry about you

getting caught, though? He must have thought it might happen."

Arnold turn his head to Evan. "Told me he'd deny everythin' if I got caught and coughed his name. Said he'd beat any charge you people tried layin' on him."

"Figures him and his lawyer buddies could wiggle him out, and he's probably right," George said in disgust.

Roger snorted. "We'll see about that."

"I wouldn' underes'imate this fellow," Arnold countered. "He's got friends in high places, or least in the right places. He also used to be a lawyer himself."

"A fine, upstanding one, too," said Roger. "A fellow to be admired.

Arnold added, "Sounded to me like Reed's got the dough and politic'l connections to pull about anythin' off. He also seems real, real set on gettin' back what he calls 'his island.'"

Roger glared at Arnold. "We'll see what he gets. We'll also see what you get out of all this, Mr. Knapp." With that he went for some air.

Amid watching Roger continue his pacings outside, Evan quietly asked, "How the heck did you get in the outhouse pit, anyway, Arnie?"

"The bench that holds the seat is broke — whole thing lifts up." Arnold grimaced. "Never should have headed for this cabin in the first place, though. Kind of worried George might know about it."

George, tongue firmly in cheek, said, "But then you would have missed out on coming clean with us."

"Yeah, that's true," said Arnold, his head pointed at his chest. "Missing that would have been a real bummer."

In a move initially surprising George and Evan, Arnold Knapp soon headed out on his own that morning. While wearily steering his boat home, Roger explained to his fellow islanders his thinking.

"If we turn him into the cops, or even just Howard, Reed would get wind soon enough and then probably high-tail it. I think we're better to let him feel all is well. That way he'll come around again and maybe we'll nail him giving Arnold more money or something. I'll have to think it through."

Gazing back at the boat's foamy wake, Evan asked, "What if Arnold tells Reed he's been caught, though?"

"I looked after that. I told Arnold before we left that if he squeals he'll not only lose his job with Howard but also be on his way to jail."

George said, "Think it registered?"

"I do."

As they neared Whisper, where the three men would soon have breakfast and catch some sleep, Evan said, "Of all the people — I never thought of Arnold. Doesn't seem like the sort someone would hire to do criminal stuff."

Roger looked at him square. "If you mean because he's a touch slow, think again. That's *exactly* why Reed chose him. In court it would be Arnold's word against his, and I wouldn't like Arnold's chances."

"So where do we go from here?" George asked.

Roger, easing off on the throttle as they approached his dock, answered, "Like I said, I'll need to set something up. At least the vandalism will stop now." Equally as confidently, he added, "We've also now got the jump on Reed."

These final words, though, he would soon retract.

George heard clearly the footsteps on his deck that Sunday afternoon, and by their distinctive pattern already surmised who was producing them. He also didn't need to let Pam in; when he reached the kitchen she was standing in the middle of it, panting from exertion.

"I've done some sleuthing of my own, and you aren't going to believe," she said, wide-eyed and beckoning George to sit with her at the table.

Turned out, soon after Roger filled her in that morning on all recent events she made a phone call. While attending Gord Ferguson's funeral back in '76 she met Katie Hanson, Nora Ferguson's niece. The two traded phone numbers and over the years had kept in touch with one another.

"Seems Reed Ferguson was awfully bitter when his parents only offered him the one lot on Whisper," Pam began. "Katie said he told her it was, quote, 'downright pathetic' he should have to share the island, and just as pathetic his parents donated the money from the other lots to their charities."

With a wry grin, George said, "They cheated him out of his rightful inheritance, in other words."

"Exactly. And can you blame them? With an attitude like that I wouldn't have left him a nickel. Anyway, it seems since he didn't get the whole island he eventually decided to abandon it altogether. That's why he sold his lot to cousin Marcy."

"And I'm betting he sold it to her because he knew Oliver's life insurance left her sitting pretty, and she was an easy target."

Pam nodded. "Apparently he found her *very* easy. Katie said he got a mitt full from Marcy for the place. Katie tried talking her out of the deal but to no avail. Marcy was convinced her dear cousin would never be dishonest with her. As for Gord and Nora, they were both far too ill at that point for Katie to get them involved."

"Reed sounds like my kind of guy," George said with a sigh. He then rose and moved to the kitchen counter. After pouring two cups of coffee, and after musing a minute, he said, "So now he evidently wants the island back, and bad. Why is that?"

Pam shrugged. "His timing is obviously connected to his retiring a few years ago. From his comments since then, though, Katie feels he has no real motive other than bitterness. She says he's made a number of nasty comments about the island and how he was cheated out of it. When I told her in confidence about Reed hiring someone to badger us she wasn't all that surprised. She also wasn't, I'm afraid, overly surprised at something else."

After delivering the coffee to the table, George said, "What's that?"

"Seems Reed has been doing more than vandalizing. He's had himself a two-fold plan."

When George's forehead creased, Pam continued with, "For quite some time, according to Katie, Reed has been bilking Marcy out of her inheritance through what he described to her as 'unlucky investments.' That's why she's been hard up for cash the last while. My guess then is this: he's doing all that bilking to basically force Marcy to sell her place. To him, of course. That way, he'll also look like her saviour!"

"He'll simply con her again, then."

"'What you can do once you can do twice' is what I'm sure he's thinking. And once he has Marcy's place he'll work on getting the rest of the island, bit by bit, as we all get fed up. He probably figures once our little community is broken up we'll just say to heck with it and start over elsewhere."

George was now shaking his head in disbelief. "Have you talked to Marcy about all this? What does she say?"

"Basically the same as she's always told Katie Hanson; that surely *Reed* would never do such a thing. 'He's such a generous fellow,' she said to me. 'Just like his father'."

George rubbed his forehead. "Poor Gord and Nora — they deserved better."

"Darn right they did, and I'm not even finished yet."

George stared at Pam, and she delivered, "Remember Marcy's upcoming family reunion? The one she's been looking forward to all summer?"

George again mulled a moment, then his face sunk into his hands. "Oh no!"

"You got it; *Reed's* idea. He's the one who proposed it, and I'm thinking that Saturday is when he intends to really lay it on thick with Marcy. What better time to get her to give him back his 'family heirloom'? Accordingly, he's built it up in Marcy's noggin as quite an event. When I took her to stock up on groceries this afternoon she told me how excited she was her family was coming to visit, and especially Reed." Waving a frustrated hand toward Marcy's place, Pam concluded with, "Her 'dear Reed,' in all his glory, is arriving for next Saturday's reunion on Friday!"

PART TWO

12

In a narrow, secluded bay at Green Heron's northwestern tip sits a small gray cottage. Overgrown and weathered it has not been visited in over twenty years. Not by a living owner, at least. Late at night teenagers sometimes dare one another to enter the long-abandoned building, and stories number many. They had seen or heard "strange things" runs the typical tale. Speculation also exists, however, that the young visitors were only imagining such things; victims, they were, of preconception. For the particular cottage in question forms the foundation of a rather historied legend on Green Heron Lake — that of the Green Heron Ghost.

If cruising Scott Bay in the summer of 1970 you would not likely have noticed anything unusual about the lake's newest and northernmost cottage, one reached only by water. Cottaging for the Logans began in typical fashion. Kim Logan — forty, divorced, and sporting a few extra bucks from a Hamilton dry cleaning business — decided it was high time she and her son had a summer getaway. In early spring of '70 she bought a remote, water-accessed lot on Green Heron and had a tiny cabin built. Although decidedly modest it sufficed, and Kim and eight-year-old Mark soon came to treasure their little retreat.

Despite her seemingly normal and pleasant cottaging

experience, most on Green Heron came to consider Kim
Logan an oddly private person. Some went further and
perceived the tall, brightly red-haired woman as downright
snobby. Little did she associate with other cottagers, even
her immediate neighbours. If you ran into her at Kirkdale's
you were lucky to receive a polite "hello," and never did she
attend the lake's annual meeting. Word also had it her life in
Hamilton wasn't much different; at work she was "most
definitely the boss," and she maintained a meagre if not
non-existent social life. As Rose Kirkdale once commented
with both sadness and puzzlement, "Other than her son she
seems to quite contentedly want no part of anyone."

In complete contrast, a forever smiling Mark Logan was
very sociable with fellow cottagers, chumming constantly
with a group of boys his age. Red-haired and tall like his
mother but far more active, he logged many a mile on Green
Heron and became both well-known and well-liked. He was
noted for being polite and uncomplaining, and also for his
goofy homemade jokes, which often were more laughed at in
pain than pleasure. ("What do you call a Canuck who does
well in school?" ... "A straight eh'er!") Alas, he was also a
story-teller occasionally guilty of embellishment, but such
were his constructive intentions no one minded. All in all,
most saw in Mark an enthusiastic, imaginative young man
with a bright future ahead.

Sadly, and largely unbeknownst to Green Heron
cottagers, Mark's life did not unfold as predicted. He may
have thrived at the lake but he withered in Hamilton. He was
clearly creative and ambitious, but the structured
environment of school didn't suit his style. As such he fared
miserably and dropped out at sixteen. What followed were
scattered, minimum-wage jobs but at these his grades proved
no better. Within several years a bright future seemed to him

highly unlikely if not entirely unattainable, and his spirits descended accordingly. Almost in tears one summer afternoon he confided to a close friend, "I just can't seem to stay on *track* with anything." His equally young friend could offer little advice, but would notice a peculiar and disturbing look in Mark's eyes on this afternoon, a look of utter confusion and desperation.

For her part, Kim Logan maintained a bullish stance, refusing to acknowledge any seriousness to her son's troubles. When Mark was still in school and teachers suggested special help, she resisted; when sympathetic employers called her prior to firing her son she contended they were the problem. "He's only going through an unfortunate phase," she continually told herself. In time all would surely pass over.

'All' came to a head, however, the summer of 1981. That year Mark, now nineteen, spent the entire season at the cottage. Recently fired from what he called "yet another pointless job" he would take a break for the summer and live on meagre savings. In the fall he'd surely find a new job, and already had a few leads. This, at least, was the telephone story he always gave his mother, who for untold reasons rarely ventured north this summer.

Truth was, Mark seemed to have anything but a plan. He was now exceedingly hyperactive and indecisive. Green Heron residents increasingly noticed a dazed excitement in his eyes, a look suggesting, as one cottager quipped, "a couple of birdies shy of a badminton set." His traditional politeness was absent — especially concerning language used in public — and his jokes were now decidedly unamusing from any angle. But, all that said, without a doubt the most startling change in Mark was a newly adopted form of recreation.

In those days a favourite hangout for younger cottagers on Green Heron, including for Mark, was a cliff on the lake's western shore named Landon Bluff. At its base are many huge, half-submerged boulders — fragments of bedrock that cleaved off to form the cliff face — and these were one attraction of the bluff. Not only did the boulders make convenient sunning and diving platforms, but behind them all manner of activities could be hidden. As the saying went on the lake, "Anything the kids shouldn't be doing they do at the bluff."

But, as may be guessed, the main attraction of Landon Bluff — for boys, at least — was the lofty perch it offered for a death-defying leap into the lake, or what was affectionately known as 'The Hop'.

At the base of the cliff, beyond the boulders, the water quickly deepens. Naturally the challenge in jumping is to launch yourself out far enough to miss the boulders and reach that deep water. Adding further interest, the top of the cliff is shaped like a set of steps, and thus offers a variety of launching points, each progressively higher and farther back from the water. You could therefore 'graduate' as your strength and nerve grew. Such had its limits, though. Dismissing the fifth and highest level, which all considered impossible, once conquering the fourth a 'Hopper' achieved his doctorate and his interest thereafter waned. So went a typical career at Landon Bluff.

Although most on Green Heron felt concern over the bluff's main activity (the issue was occasionally raised at lake meetings), no cottager ever put forward a serious effort to stop it. The fact was that no kid had ever been hurt, and so most maintained crossed fingers and a "boys will be boys" view of the matter. Mind, this stance assumed the adherence to certain boundaries.

In that summer of 1981, in what almost had to be seen to be truly believed, Mark Logan started jumping from the fifth and highest level at Landon Bluff.

At first friends found it quite a thrill and even egged him on. This was "cutting edge," the birth of a whole new rank among Hoppers, and soon only "wussies" wouldn't be following suit. None, though, ever did, and watching Mark merely once showed you why. Despite a frenzied launch run and eardrum-bursting yell he always just barely made it beyond the farthest Landon boulder. As friends nervously joked, if wearing one size of shorts larger he'd have grazed the boulder. It was that close.

Kim Logan received the first phone call to her Hamilton home in early July. Tracy Spence, who at least managed a few short chats with Kim over the years, was concerned.

"I wanted to talk to you about Mark," she said tenderly after several minutes of introductory weather analysis. "I'm sorry for being nosy; I realize you and I don't know one another well. But Mark's been acting very ... oddly this summer, and I felt you should be notified."

"And what do you consider odd?" came a stern reply.

"I'm afraid he's been very reckless."

"He's always been goofy at the lake."

"Yes, I realize, but not necessarily reckless. Things have developed to the point where people around the lake are getting pretty worried. Regarding Landon Bluff especially. Mark has been really taking major chan—"

"Why, might I ask, would they be so worried?"

In responding Tracy stumbled a moment, but then offered, "Because ... we care about him, Kim."

"You *care* about him?" Kim uttered the words, Tracy later claimed, in utter disbelief. Too, as she basically had in Hamilton so many times she soon ended the conversation with, "There's nothing at all wrong with my son. Please carry on with your own affairs."

This proved the first of a handful of calls to Kim that summer. Jim Forrest, Patty Noel, and Rhonda Boyer all made attempts — sometimes desperate — to convince the Logan mother her son had problems. Conversations always concluded, however, with the same essential message: Kim wanted no part of anyone's "input." Also, no one ever saw her visit Green Heron to investigate her son's reported behaviour.

To most the end result was inevitable. On a sunny morning in late August, about a week before the Labour Day weekend, Mark Logan failed to clear the farthest boulder at Landon Bluff. Witnesses said the result was nothing less than gruesome, and when police and ambulance personnel arrived at the scene none doubted a young man had lost his life. Adding further emphasis to the day, no accounts exist of anyone — not even the most brazen — ever jumping from the bluff again.

Mark's funeral was held in Hamilton two days after his fateful leap, with many Green Heron cottagers attending. Flanked by several she hardly knew, Kim Logan laid her one and only child to rest. Immediately after the funeral, however, she forever parted company from almost all who attended.

She had an extremely long and lonely winter that year. In mid-January she turned over all control of the dry cleaning business to her lead employee, supposedly temporarily, but considering her state few expected her back. She now hardly lifted her head over the course of a day. And when in May she forced herself to the cottage her condition only worsened.

During her stay at the lake many of the same cottagers

who begged her attention the previous summer visited in an effort to console, but they made little progress. Unlike with the phone calls Kim did not reject these efforts, but she was hopelessly lost in grief. Regret, too, haunted her. As one visitor later commented, "She's completely convinced that not listening to the world around her cost her a son, and it's a tough conviction to counter. As annoyed as I was last summer, I really feel sorry for her now, and worry dearly for her."

That worry unfortunately prove founded.

Apparently unable to start her motor, Kim Logan was last spotted rowing her aged tin boat that spring, her unkempt red hair harshly noticeable against a black leather jacket. Soon after she also apparently proceeded to scuttle the boat and drown herself by some means, because none of her family or employees in Hamilton ever saw her again.

One basic fact, though, countered this presumption of suicide: neither her boat or body were ever found, despite an extensive search by police divers. This naturally raised debate: was she really deceased? Some suggested that on the day last seen she reached the mainland, returned to the city (her car was missing from the marina), then moved overseas to start a new life. As for her boat, so withdrawn was Kim that three weeks passed before relatives reported her missing, and in such time, left abandoned, some kids might well have 'borrowed it.'

This alternate theory concerning her fate largely dissolved, however, the spring of 1983.

Dorothy Burke, her voice quavering and her hands trembling, made her report to both police and witnesses alike: she had seen Kim Logan that morning.

There was no mistaking her — the red hair, the black leather jacket, the aged rowboat; "Who else could it have been?" Dorothy was enjoying a dawn stroll near Ferg Landing when out of the lake mist Kim appeared in her boat. Dorothy immediately called to her but received no answer. Not even a glance. Kim merely stared off into the distance, searchingly and in seeming agony.

That incident proved only the beginning.

Not all were taken seriously. In July of 1985 a nearsighted Ellen Stewart reported seeing Kim "from a rather considerable distance." The following year police received an anonymous call from several boaters claiming they'd come upon a drifting rowboat "that had creaky oarlocks and a creepy, ghostly feel about it." And in July of 1993 John Jarvis claimed he not only saw but had a short chat with a passing Kim Logan as he sat fishing mid-lake. Unfortunately for Mr. Jarvis a healthy supply of refreshments discovered onboard effectively nullified that report.

But then there were those given great credibility. When in 1991 Howard Kirkdale stated he had witnessed a red-haired woman in a black jacket ("but not *necessarily* Kim Logan") rowing an aged tin boat ("but not *necessarily* Kim's"), eyebrows of even the most staunch disbelievers rose slightly. No-nonsense to his core, Howard Kirkdale was not considered prone to delusion or fibbing, and his account seemed a touch too coincidental.

The 'crème de la crème' sighting, however, undoubtedly came in 1995 courtesy of Stan Milne, George Clarke's favourite person. Some found his evidence staggering: a photograph. It showed, from a distance of about thirty yards, a red-haired, black-jacketed woman of Kim Logan's height and figure rowing a small boat through light mist, with Green Heron clearly identified by Fred Banner's cottage in the background.

Immediately some questioned its validity, citing how "proper, genuine ghosts" traditionally fail to appear in photographs. But if the individual depicted just happened, in an incredible fluke, to match the Green Heron Ghost profile, then who was this person? No one ever came forward. And was Stan's picture a fake, then? Respected or otherwise on the lake you only had to look in his eyes to see he was not pulling a prank. He was extremely shaken up by the whole incident, and he and Mary Milne were absent on the lake for over a year afterward.

All told, one observation common in reports was the apparent mood of this mysterious rowing figure. Most witnesses contended this was not an angry person but rather one ashamed and deeply grieving. Kim Logan's was not a spiteful ghost, that is, but one "unable to rest through deep regret."

Media attention was perhaps inevitable. In 1996 a magazine did a feature article on the Green Heron Ghost. A reporter from *Haunted Haven* spent three full days interviewing cottagers and watching for the ghost at dawn. She had great success with the former but none with the latter, and many wondered whether she left the lake truly convinced. Regardless, the article, 'Ghost at Green Heron: Are you a Believer?' appeared in the magazine's April issue, complete with Stan Milne's famous photograph, and undoubtedly every cottager on the lake has a copy tucked away.

That article essentially chiselled the legend into stone

for the lake's cottagers. Believer or not, you couldn't deny the ghost was a "bona fide issue." Accordingly, during the years following yet more sightings were reported, and equally as many speculations offered concerning their credibility. And obviously, the legend was classic material for a late night campfire story.

George Clarke's rendition of the tale was either the most famous or infamous, depending on who you talked to. Whisper seemed the perfect setting for the story, out as you were in the middle of the lake on a tiny island. George always put forth a full effort and was usually rewarded with several sleepless listeners. In this he found endless entertainment, non-believer that he was.

This, at least, he forever contended.

One June morning in 1992 he woke early to the sound of his shed door repeatedly banging. Through the bedroom window he saw a storm was moving in, one catching him by surprise, and it was heralded by gusting winds.

After shutting the cottage's screened windows he put on slippers and stepped out to close the shed door, which he accidentally left open the previous evening. The day was still dim under a heavily-clouded sky and also cool. As he walked he shivered slightly.

It was just after he closed the shed door and turned the latch that off to his left he heard grating, creaking sounds. They struck George as much like those made by a rusty hinge, or perhaps more like several. At first he thought it might be another door. The sounds, however, seemed to be coming from the lake.

Creeping toward shore he peered out into the mist, which was especially thick this morning. He saw nothing and yet the sounds continued. Moving to the very edge of shore he put one hand on a tree and leaned out, trying to see farther down the lake. Still nothing in sight and the sounds were now fading; whatever the source it was slowly moving away. Save for the wind gusting through the trees, within a minute all was again quiet.

To this day George has never entirely settled in his mind what made those sounds that cool, dreary June morning. He decided against making inquiries with his fellow cottagers. What he did do, known only to himself, was return inside, sit at the kitchen table with coffee, and gaze an hour out at the lake, vacantly.

13

The last two weeks of August comprise a traditionally hallowed time on Whisper Island. Since their fourth season together the islanders have always taken their summer holidays together, and the last two weeks of August became the agreed upon period. This was, as Pam put it, a time of "really digging into the cottage"; one of parties, midnight swims, goofy spending sprees in Birchport, and quiet reflection. The islanders thus often went to great lengths to ensure their presence. Although some claimed he'd likely be "sent onward" soon anyway, Evan Dean even quit a job one summer so he could attend Whisper these two summer weeks. They were considered that precious.

Unfortunately, the outset of 2002's summer holidays was not celebrated with the usual enthusiasm. Indeed it was not celebrated in the least, for soon after "all hands were on deck" the evening of Friday, August 23rd, the one and only Reed Ferguson arrived.

As a favour to Marcy, Pam shuttled him to the island from Ferg Landing. During that cruise she was tempted to 'eliminate the problem' right then and there. But she managed, for Marcy's sake, to keep her cool, and after dropping Reed at his cousin's dock she even waved mechanically while pulling away. Soon, however, she proceeded to viciously slam the boat into her own dock. Vented frustrations continued with a hearty round of cursing.

Leaving Marcy time to provide Reed with his supper, Roger later paid a visit to supposedly "get clear on a few details" regarding the following day's family reunion. When he reached Marcy's he found Reed ensconced in a deck chair, smoking a pipe while reading the day's paper.

Other than Marcy, none of the islanders had laid eyes on Reed Ferguson since the funerals of his parents, the second of which (his mother's) was in 1977. He had not attended the ceremonial release of Gord and Nora's ashes on Whisper's headland. In terms of actually speaking with him, however, Roger had to reflect back even further than the Fergusons' funerals — to the August afternoon in 1973 he bought the Whisper lot. That day Reed had privately offered some snide remarks concerning the purchaser's wisdom, and also a few concerning the worthiness of the charity receiving the sale's proceeds. Roger had largely dismissed these comments, but he did remember well Reed's expression — a heartless, superior grin that contrasted starkly with his father's.

Some thirty-two years later, that same annoying grin was the first thing Roger noticed when approaching Reed on Marcy's deck. His hair may have become entirely gray and much less abundant, his weight might have increased forty or so pounds, but this was clearly the same Reed Ferguson.

"What's new in the news?" Roger asked with a very forced smile, immediately granting himself the chair across from Reed's.

"Not a whole lot. Some of my stocks are up, though. I like seeing that." Reed pulled his pipe from his mouth. "Haven't seen you in a long, long time, lad. How are you?"

"I'm holding up. We've wound up enjoying the island a

lot more than I remember you predicting. We're still here."

"Yes, I'd noticed that. Marcy has mentioned about you and Pam many times. And George and Evan. You've developed into quite a close-knit group, too, I understand."

"Delighted to announce we have."

"As thick as thieves, you are."

Roger offered a harsh glare. He wanted to add, "We didn't steal this island from your inheritance, your self-centeredness stole it from you," but restrained himself.

Instead, Reed continued with, "So I heard through Marcy you've been having troubles on the island."

"We have. And still are, for that matter — all kinds of troubles. Just last week some kind soul decided to scrape clean his boots with our TV screen."

Calmly, Reed said, "You don't say? I'm real sorry to hear that. What's the deal — kids horsing around?"

"*Somebody* horsing around."

Roger watched closely, but Reed showed no sign of alarm. His eyes didn't widen, and his newspaper didn't tremble in the slightest. Classic signs of a true criminal, Roger thought to himself.

"Have ... the police made any progress?"

Roger shrugged. "Not really. Your — (he almost said "your boy") ... the *guy* has been real tidy with fingerprints and whatnot. I can report this, though — whoever it is he'd better hope the police catch him first."

It was right after delivering this veiled threat that Roger at last noticed a reaction in Reed. The Ferguson son took a somewhat stronger draw on his pipe than normal, and through the subsequent smoke he stared at Roger coldly. Within a few seconds, however, he pulled his pipe away, beamed again that standard smug grin, and said, "Well ... don't look at *me*."

"Are you sure, Reed?" Roger said with a chuckle amid rising, pretending to share in the joke. But soon at Marcy's door he whispered to himself, ""We'll see about that grin."

As commanded by a pacing wife, Roger filed a report immediately upon returning from Marcy's. He delivered it sitting at the kitchen table, and before Pam even allowed him coffee.

"The first thing I'll tell you is this," Roger began. "He's on to us. I haven't figured out how, but he knows we know about him."

"You're sure?"

"I'm sure. I finally got a rise out of him when we were talking about the vandalism. He fought a good fight, but in the end gave himself away."

Running her fingers lovingly through her husband's hair, Pam said, "Poor thing didn't stand a chance against my Rogey."

"Darn right he didn't."

"Think Arnold squealed, then?

"No, I don't. I'll interrogate Kirkdale's overachiever on that front, but I think Reed just somehow keeps his ear to the ground around the lake, or has someone keep an ear for him. True, to prevent Reed from suspecting us we've been spreading news the vandalism's still going on, but obviously we haven't been calling the police anymore. Word of that change may have gotten to him."

"And yet knowing we know, he still shows up here?!"

Roger smiled and nodded. "If that surprises you, honey,

wait till you see the perpetual look on this guy's face. He's as cocky as they come."

Pam said, "So what now, then?"

"I say — for Marcy's sake, at least — we maintain a polite face, and play the game one step at a time. Hope, too, that whatever Mr. Clarke next door has up his sleeve is a winner."

"What *George* has up his sleeve?"

Roger eyed Pam. "Don't ask me what, but he's developed a scheme, that boy. The last couple of times I've talked to him it's been like talking to Reed — you get the distinct impression you're not getting the straight goods. I assume with George, though, it's for a good reason."

Pam's forehead creased. "Come to think of it, Marcy's been sort of ... *funny* with me the last week, if it's possible, that is, for her to be any more that way. Think George has her in on this little scheme?"

"God only knows," said Roger, "I'm guessing by the end of tomorrow, though, we'll know."

About eleven that evening, after three failed attempts at retiring, a wound up Marcy brought a piece of peach pie to Reed, now reading in her living room. The dessert — his favourite — was from a pie made specially for him. Marcy had inquired by phone earlier in the week about all her cousin's favourites, which he clearly listed.

Setting the pie on the coffee table before him, Marcy said, "By the way, did you have a nice chat with Roger earlier? Isn't he wonderful?"

"Yes. Absolutely. Everyone who's made a home on my

island is wonderful."

"Your island?"

"Just kidding, dear. But you know — it sometimes feels like it still is my island. Or should be. All those years here ..." Reed now looked solemnly to the window, to Whisper's moonlit shore. A moment later he glanced at Marcy, and her moistened eyes confirmed his desired effect.

"Maybe, then, you should have stayed, Reed. I'm thankful for you graciously selling me this cottage, but —"

"Maybe it would be to our mutual benefit," Reed broke in, "if it changed hands again. I'd get my cottage back, and you'd rid yourself of money problems. I think we'd both win, but especially you." Softening his voice, Reed added, "And you know how deeply I care about you."

Marcy's face brightened. "You're such an angel! I don't know what I'd do without you!"

"You might have to do without me, by what I've heard."

"What do you mean?"

"All the vandalism on the island? Roger Marsden thinks it's been me."

"Been you?! Why would it —?"

Reed smiled. "Again, just *kidding*."

"Oh you! You're a little devil! I should have known, of course. My neighbours would never think like that — heavens no! They're all the nicest people, and they've helped me too much over the years to keep this cottage. I'm so glad we're together."

With that Marcy headed off for bed again, and therefore didn't hear Reed's final remark. "Not for long, dear," he said, starting in on his pie. "Not for long."

14

"It's really quite simple," red-haired Teresa Ferguson would patiently explain to a red-haired granddaughter. "Immediately after a date you retire to your room and lie backwards on your bed. You rest your right foot — and *right* foot only — on your reading pillow and place the tip of your left forefinger on the very tip of your nose. With your right hand you then bounce the lid from his box of chocolates off the ceiling, going easy on the plaster. If the lid lands with the label up, and his dinner tie clashed with your dress, you've found your fellow."

After such advice the granddaughter always apologetically returned, with a hand masking a smile, "I'm sorry, Grandma, but ... none of it makes any sense to me."

Such a response similarly always brought forth a sly glance, capped with, "And so it goes from there."

Marcy Donnell was twenty-two when she truly began discerning the light at the end of her grandmother's tunnel. Although never actually taking the elder Donnell's advice, the utterly irrational nature of life's bonds more than displayed itself through her found fellow.

When Marcy went on her first date with Oliver Willett, most believed she was simply making a "statement." Raised

in a struggling farming family Oliver was dirt poor, coarsely
mannered, and ill-educated. In contrast, with Marcy's father
a prominent Toronto lawyer, her family lived lavishly. She
would, without hesitation, sit down to the most formal of
dinner parties. And in school, Marcy was considered a
prodigy. She graduated from her five-year collegiate
program at a record age of sixteen, earned a B.A. by
eighteen, and received a doctorate in sociology at age
twenty-three. In doing so, none contended Marcy's
scholastic achievements were merely prompted by her
family's resources and influence. You only needed to look in
Marcy Donnell's eyes to see she was a highly perceptive,
ambitious, and talented young lady.

Why, then, Marcy showed an interest in Oliver Willett
none knew. Her parents certainly objected to their pairing,
and among her girl friends she was often teased. One even
predicted a future movie, a horror-tragedy in all likelihood:
"Lady Einstein meets Farmer Joe."

Marcy first met Oliver when the two were forcibly
paired at an autumn fair in 1958, a year after she earned her
doctorate. Accompanied by four girl friends, all standing
ahead of her, Marcy stood in line waiting to board a Ferris
wheel. When her group reached the entry gate and the
operator insisted the ride only allowed two per seat — and
also no less — Marcy soon found herself seated beside one
Oliver Willett.

Although she had never previously spoken with the
sinewy, earthy-haired young man, who was one year her
senior, she did already know a few things about him. This by
way of a group of farmers — Oliver's father included — once
having a land dispute with the government and hiring
Marcy's father to represent them (successfully). Marcy knew
Oliver was quite poor, had asthma, had left school at fifteen,

and, curiously, was a frequent entertainer for ill and disadvantaged children. This final item was what most intrigued her.

"So what sort of things do you do to please the children," she asked even before they'd completed their first revolution.

"I play some harmonica tunes, tell jokes, and sometimes I juggle."

"You juggle? Where did you learn to do that?"

"From a farm hand we once had, back when pa could afford one."

"So you juggle balls?"

Oliver shook his head. "Nope — mainly juggle horseshoes."

"Horseshoes?! Go on! They're too heavy. Surely no one juggles *horseshoes*."

"Wanna bet?"

Marcy smiled. Feeling daring, she said, "*Maybe* — what's the bet?"

"If I juggle some horseshoes for say ... one minute, you'll be my date at the fair."

"And if you can't?"

"Then I'll be *your* date at the fair."

Marcy tittered a moment, but then said "sure," thinking all this surely a joke.

What she didn't realize was that the small sack Oliver brought with him onto the Ferris wheel had three horseshoes in it. Seems he'd earlier used them in the fair's tournament. She also didn't expect he'd win his bet right then and there.

So it was a large crowd soon formed that evening to watch Oliver Willett juggle horseshoes a full minute on a rocking-seated Ferris wheel. And, while a prominent lawyer's daughter almost died from a combination of intense fear he'd drop one (which he didn't), and laughter.

'And so it goes from there ...'

They married only a year later, but not without considerable dissent. On exactly seven lengthy sessions before the wedding Marcy listened to her parents inform her "she was throwing her life away."

"What if you wind up *pregnant*?" her mother demanded, shuddering. "Keep that in mind, young lady — if you buy a house you can always sell it, but once you have children, *you have children*. This mistake would become entirely irreversible."

But Marcy persevered, and following their wedding the couple began a life together. Ottawa remained their home for their first three years. Tired of certain disapproving parents, the couple then bought a house in Kitchener. Marcy wished to remain at least somewhat in her parents' good graces, however, and so begged of Oliver they hold off a few years longer before having children. "A kid should have two grandmothers," she suggested with a smile. "Let's wait until both come around."

Marcy woke early the morning of Saturday, October 26, 1963. Oliver was making "funny noises," and in her half sleep she told him so. Ten minutes passed before she fully awakened and realized her husband's noises hadn't ceased.

"What's the matter?"

"With what?"

Marcy turned on her side and scowled. "With you? Your

breathing sounds horrible."

"It's nothin'. Go back to sleep."

"I'll decide what's nothing. Did you take your asthma medication?"

"Yes, I did."

Marcy sat up. "You're sure —?" She broke off, because she could now better see Oliver. Not only was his breathing laboured, he was pale and sweaty.

Oliver peered at her shocked stare. "What?"

In a commanding force, and immediately leaving the bed, Marcy said, "You're going to the hospital."

She dressed quickly, but not frantically. Oliver had long experienced occasional problems with his asthma, and presently suffering from a cold such occurrences were normal. Still, they would be cautious.

He proved anything but fine.

Shortly after they arrived at the emergency ward of the local hospital a doctor informed Marcy that Oliver had fluid in his lungs, then "Considering his asthma, we're transferring him to Toronto General."

Rather than ride in the ambulance with Oliver, Marcy decided to follow in the car. Who knew, after all, how long Oliver would be in the hospital in Toronto? If she'd be staying with her parents for a spell, she'd need the car.

Traffic was not overly heavy on this day as they drove out of the city. Soon enough, however, several cars and a transport truck came between Marcy and the ambulance, which drove without its siren on. Worse, she soon had to stop for nearly a minute while the transport in front of her backed into a parking lot. The ambulance, meanwhile, kept going.

She knew it was silly to panic — she knew how to get to Toronto General on her own — but she somewhat did nonetheless. Somehow losing sight of the ambulance made it seem she was losing Oliver. She therefore elected to turn off onto a side street, quickly scoot south, and reconnect with the ambulance on what she figured was its route.

But Marcy could not explain later why she travelled where she did that morning. Was it traffic? Did she believe this route quicker? She could not say for sure. She did recall being upset, and in the end, concluded this was why she didn't even see the ambulance until broadsiding it.

She regained consciousness some six hours later. The walls and sheets of the hospital room seemed almost too white, and before her head entirely cleared she wondered that she'd already reached the next world. But then came the voice of a nurse, and soon her and another were standing beside her bed. "How ... did I wind up in here?" was her first question. Her second concerned Oliver.

His funeral was held the following Monday. It rained that day, a misty drizzle that soaked everyone attending the cemetery service. This atmosphere reflected well what lay within Mary Willett — to lose a husband was one thing, but in this fashion? She was already haunted by guilt.

Her parents sympathized, naturally — they were not quite that cruel concerning Oliver. But they also unquestionably saw an opportunity for their daughter to make a fresh start. Perhaps not tomorrow, or next month, but in due time she would find someone new and begin life anew. Someone, too, a touch more "appropriate."

That did not happen. Now living with her parents Marcy, slowly but surely, fell apart. When six months had passed, and Christine Donnell could not remember the last time her daughter had even stepped outside, she decided professional help was required. The net result of that move, however, was more than Marcy stepping outside. She left altogether.

William Donnell was away and unavailable at this time. Short his legal advice, Christine reacted by calling the police. She suggested Marcy be "taken ... *into custody*," to which she heard the following:

"I'm very sorry, Mrs. Donnell, but it's not against the law to be mentally ill in this country. If Marcy doesn't wish to enter an institution, and she does not break any laws, she's free to do as she pleases."

Christine had a difficult time accepting this particular 'rule' of society. But if her ill daughter so badly wanted to go out on her own, and had every legal right to do so, then so be it. May the good lord go with her.

From that day in 1965 Marcy effectively fended for herself the next ten years. How she managed to do so became, for her Kitchener landlord, shopkeepers and assorted others she interacted with, a complete mystery. Luckily, her father had insisted Oliver take out a sizable life insurance policy, so she was fine for money. In addition, she became very miserly; she wore clothes, for example, until they were threadbare before replacing them. Her one allowed luxury was her "glorious flowers," which she maintained in numerous beds in her landlord's backyard. Singing to herself, and sometimes even dancing, she would dabble for hours at a time in the yard. The landlord and neighbours couldn't help notice her peculiar gardening style, and in her neighbourhood she became known as "Whimsy Willett."

Her hair loss began in 1967. First in bits, then in clumps,

her once rich, shiny red hair came out. Within a year she was essentially bald. Not far into this process she took to wearing wigs, and actually had fun with them; soon enough she had an assortment numbering nearly a dozen. She kept them neatly arranged on styrofoam heads in her closet, and even had a name for each, although these she kept private. Some things, after all, could only be between her and Oliver.

And so life went for Marcy. For years each day passed almost indiscernibly from that previous. Only occasionally was her daily pattern broken, such as when her father died of a heart attack in 1970. At other times family matters again broke the monotony of her life, such as when her mother called. But for the most part Marcy existed within the tiny bubble of her apartment and gardens; although she still cherished family ties, almost always she avoided contact, inventing polite excuses as necessary.

One family gathering she did attend, following numerous pleas by phone, was the wedding of Katie Hanson, her sister Brenda's eldest daughter. The event was held in autumn of 1975, a week before Thanksgiving. It was Marcy's first wedding "since the turn of the century," and when she at last treated herself to a new dress. The wedding was also, unfortunately, when many relatives and old friends discovered just how far "down the rabbit hole" Marcy had descended.

Among them was Reed Ferguson.

Although cousins, Marcy had not spent much time during childhood with Reed, the youngest son of her mother's brother, Gord Ferguson. Despite adoring his generous, kind-hearted parents, Marcy did not care for Master Ferguson. He struck her as selfish, conceited, and domineering; to play any game with this cousin was to be constantly informed of "the official rules," which he naturally

devised and adjusted to his benefit as the game progressed.
Marcy thus went out of her way to avoid him, including
never visiting his family's cottage on Green Heron Lake.

But that perception of Reed, of course, was something
that existed "way back then," as Marcy would tell him. And
somehow she couldn't quite remember well that former era.
All she really knew at present was that Reed was family,
looked much like his father, and seemed very pleasant.

At the wedding Reed quickly saw Marcy was now
'challenged,' and that she obviously cherished family and
therefore trusted him implicitly. Add to that his knowledge
of her deep pockets via Oliver's life insurance, and she
became for him a veritable dream come true.

Disgusted his parents were leaving him only a quarter of
Whisper Island — which with a bulldozer he saw great
potential in — Reed bitterly choose to abandon the family
cottage altogether. That decision was only reinforced upon
learning cousin Marcy was ripe for the picking. In surely the
real estate deal of the century on Green Heron, Reed
ultimately received (extracted) from Marcy almost three
times his inherited property's appraised value. This despite a
concerted effort by the newly-wed Katie Hanson to prevent
the transaction. Katie's hands, however, were effectively tied.
Not only did Marcy refuse to believe Reed was cheating her,
but with Gord and Nora Ferguson now quite ill, Katie
couldn't bring herself to try getting them to intervene. The
dear Fergusons, she figured, didn't need to leave this world
with tainted fond memories of their beloved island.

So, in November of 1975, Marcy Willett became the
proud owner of a cottage on Whisper Island. Excited beyond
measure, after several unsuccessful excursions she finally
boarded a bus headed for the village of Birchport. She then
took a water taxi from Green Heron's sole marina to

Whisper Island. There, after gazing upon a cottage she had purchased with no more knowledge of than it being a cottage, she delightedly set about planting some flowers. That was the snowy day, as previously mentioned, Pam Marsden met her.

Thankfully, there was a bright side to Marcy's cottaging experience, and that proved Whisper's community. To begin, seeing Marcy heading to and from the island in an expensive water taxi, Pam and Roger Marsden were quick to offer her a seat in their boat. So too a seat in their car upon learning she faced a "simply wonderful four-hour bus trip" to and from Toronto, connection layovers not included. Lastly, a year after Marcy acquired her cottage the Marsdens offered her their basement apartment (at a rent rate that lost the couple money). This simplified Marcy's trips to Whisper even further. The apartment also gained for Marcy several protective friends, which she obviously dearly needed.

That said, it would be the help and companionship of George Clarke that would prove Marcy's most treasured acquisition upon joining Whisper. Mind, the 'help' component of their relationship would be almost all their fellow islanders recognized. No doubting, to Pam and Roger especially, that George tended to every 'masculine' chore, large and small, that popped up at Marcy's place. Listening to him invent many more such chores also left no doubt in their minds he had something of a crush on Marcy. But what these fellow islanders did not see — despite George's several attempts at explanation — was that he and Marcy somehow connected in a curious and special way.

With George, Marcy Willett sometimes had 'moments of clarity.' In a similar way to that often professed by those suffering from alcoholism, Marcy would sometimes — for as little as several minutes — become her former self again.

And since that former self had a doctorate under its belt, the contrast was often enough to virtually knock George Clarke out of his chair.

The first such experience George had with Marcy was on a June day in 1977. George had just finished repairing Marcy's water pump and the two were seated at her kitchen table for lunch.

During their conversation Marcy spoke of an issue raised at a recent Green Heron Lake Association meeting, one the islanders together attended. A cottager proposed greater restrictions on the removal of shoreline trees, and his remark sparked quite heated debate. From Marcy, in light of her initial words on this topic, George expected yet more off the wall comments.

Standing before her open refrigerator, however, Marcy said, "I do not necessarily maintain a specific position on this issue, but I categorically object to the manner of its debate. For neighbours to hurl vicious, personal insults at one another is not a constructive approach to problem solving. Each individual or party presenting their position — in turn — in a clear, calm manner would surely prove much more productive."

George only stared dumbfounded at Marcy after her outburst, while she merely returned to rooting through the fridge. Too, before he could make inquires, Marcy gazed blandly toward the kitchen window and said, "My word! The clouds are rolling in! Although, I don't think they really roll, do they, George? Why do people always say that? I don't think clouds have *wheels* on them. Have to be pretty big ones ..." And on she went as normal.

When George shared his experience that same evening with Roger and Pam, they merely snickered. Apparently they supposed that for George, in his romantically blinded state,

Marcy was becoming a little larger than life. It was all similar, they judged, to a teenaged girl 'seeing' her heartthrob of a boyfriend lift a car out of a ditch. And that's what the Marsdens figured would be the equivalent of George's claimed feat. Never had they witnessed any such miraculous transformation in Marcy, and being her landlord and means of transportation they'd spent far more time with her than George.

So, when it came down to George merely being teased when mentioning Marcy's special moments, he stopped mentioning them. As the years passed and those moments became almost countless for George, he thus gained a closeness with Marcy his fellow islanders never fully understood. Similarly others on Green Heron, who George several times heard wondering aloud if the real thing he 'fixed' for Marcy was her bank account. Or perhaps something else she had to offer. But George would only ignore such speculation, self-assured that the purely platonic relationship he and Marcy maintained was nothing but a blessing for both of them.

Not only did George feel Marcy regained the dignity of her former self during her 'awakenings,' but also he often found himself learning from and inspired by her remarks. This was perhaps most true on an August evening in 1998. That weekend both Evan and the Marsdens were away, leaving George and Marcy on their own for a traditional 'sunsetter.' This, of course, they nonetheless still enjoyed at the view-advantaged Marsdens'.

Among their conversation topics, which Marcy typically changed by the minute, George mentioned a recent visit by Tom and Dorothy Burke — the couple who owned the cottage near Ferg Landing. As they had several times in past, they inquired with George about why he and fellow cottagers had remained on such a "wanting" island all these years. They were not necessarily being critical, George sensed, simply curious.

He mentioned this to Marcy — not really expecting a response — purely to vent frustration, although he was puzzled why he felt that frustration. Turned out, Marcy of all people helped him with that problem.

George had not quite finished his account of his conversation with the Burkes when 'the voice,' as he had come to call it, interrupted him.

"Sadly, George," Marcy began, "What some people don't see is that our community is not one of five, but one of six."

By now not nearly so shocked at Marcy's transformations, George calmly said, "'Fraid I don't follow. Who's number six?"

"I believe a community is an assembly of living elements which coexist and, most notably, interact. The latter means you as a member affect, and are affected by, other members." With sparkling eyes Marcy now added, "Number six, for me, is Whisper Island itself."

George mulled this over a moment, then said, "Can't remember the island banging any nails into my cottage for me."

"No, but it's done many other things for you — it's given back to you a taste of the woods you lost after moving to the city. Maybe you've forgotten that influence, and why the Burkes have frustrated you without your even understanding why."

George's eyebrows rose slightly over this insight, but Marcy only continued.

"You're not alone, either. The island has helped settle Evan, it's helped shelter me from the evils of the world, and it's somehow inspired Pam — a few times I've witnessed her out at dawn, seemingly trying to run. So as I see it, the island is as much a member of the community as any person. *That's* why Whisper is so dear to us, and why we've all stayed here so long.

George remained quiet now, and Marcy soon concluded with, "For me, the universe is comprised of the earth, the stars, and this island, George. This wonderful island friend whose community includes itself."

15

Marcy woke about five on Saturday, August 24, 2002. Immediately slipping from bed she went to her window and feverishly pulled back the drapes. It was still dark, but gazing upward she nonetheless gained evidence of the day to come: a star-filled sky. "Thank *goodness!*" she whispered before delightedly prancing to her closet. And so began for Marcy her cherished family reunion.

Pam Marsden started her day about a half hour later, and despite striving to rise silently she still woke Roger.

"What's all this?" he groggily inquired, glancing at a lighted clock.

Continuing to dress, Pam answered matter-of-factly, "Slowing down Marcy."

In truth she had two items on her agenda. Not only would she need to restrain Marcy from having supper ready by 9:00 a.m, she figured the less time Reed spent alone with his cousin the better. He'd gone to considerable trouble setting up his little 'con weekend,' so likely he'd make the most of it.

Her hunch proved correct; when she soon tapped on Marcy's door Reed opened it within seconds. Further reinforcing her notion, he did not exactly greet her with a warm, welcoming smile. So encouraged, Pam cheerily offered, "Just come to help my sweetie!" then lovingly squeezed her way inside.

With Reed muttering something and disappearing into the guest bedroom, Pam set about fulfilling her second mission. Her prediction concerning Marcy also proved accurate; sporting torn slacks, one sock, and her "marigold mania" house robe, she already had seemingly every pot, dish, and cooking utensil she owned scattered about her kitchen counter and table. She divided her attention between this chaos and that in her bedroom, where similarly all manner of clothes were spread over her bed. Conversation (if that's what it was) played out accordingly. "What do you think — the silver blouse or the blue? By the way, have you seen my crock pot? Did you borrow it, dear? If you did you're perfectly welcome, but while you're fetching it could you please make up your mind about the blouse? But oh my! I should be in the bath, don't you think?" After fifteen minutes worth of "slowing down Marcy" Pam defeatedly sat herself in a kitchen chair. A long day apparently lay ahead.

Soon enough the remainder of Marcy's guests began arriving at Ferg Landing. The task of delivering them to the island was Roger's, and about nine-thirty he embarked on the first of many runs to the mainland. With him on that first run was Evan, who volunteered to serve as the landing's parking attendant.

Roger and Evan knew few in Marcy's family. Both had met merely a handful of those attending the funerals for Gord and Nora Ferguson. They did their best to memorize names on a list the host provided, however, and endeavoured to be warm and 'colourful' in their assigned chores. When the four piece band arrived, for instance, Roger had them play Marcy's all-time favourite — 'Moon River' — as they approached the dock, which pleased her to no end. She even did a little dance, earning herself a hearty round of applause.

For his part, George was the "grounds manager." He devoted himself to setting up tables and chairs, and tending to forty-seven other "essentials" Marcy brought to his attention. Soon enough, though, guests became avid helpers and he was able to take a break. At this time he headed to Marcy's fridge for some drinking water. Close by he found Pam, briefly alone, doing the first of many loads of dishes.

"Can you *believe* him, George?" she said quietly but scornfully, pointing out the kitchen window at Reed, who through all preparations and festivities had remained seated at a picnic table. "You know — I haven't seen him even take a walk around Marcy's lot yet, let alone tour the island. He doesn't care about this place; there's no bond. It's exactly like Katie Hanson said — who by the way, refused to come today. He only wants this island because he bitterly figures it should be his." Pam all but spit into her dishwater. "Reminds me of a five-year-old boy tugging a toy he doesn't even like away from another kid *'cause it's mine!'* That's about the level this guy's at."

Following this outburst, George grinned. "I'm amazed he's still alive at this point, all considering. Roger told me you've been over here since hour one."

"Oh, I've been here, all right. Vulnerable Marcy certainly can't be left alone for long with someone like that. As far as allowing him to continue breathing, don't count on it."

"Here, *here*," George said with a sigh. "Don't worry about this Reed character. I say we focus on the day — make it as nice an affair for Marcy as we can."

"Yes! I agree! But you have to remember this whole 'affair,' as you call it, is part of *his* little scheme. I just finished making two gigantic salads, for instance, to forward his stupid plot *against us*. It's insane!"

"No. You made salads to please Marcy's true guests. Forget about Reed."

Ignoring this, Pam continued with, "The really tough part — the agonizing part — is that he's built this reunion into such a gigantic thing in Marcy's head. That way we can't touch him, you see; that's his armour. Confronting him would make a big scene and spoil Marcy's dream weekend, and likely she'd never forgive us. He's got us in a trap, and he knows it." Looking like she was ready to toss a plate through the window, Pam finished with, "God I'd love to wipe that smirk off his face."

"Me too, but for now I've decided to just smile at him. Yes ma'am — 'Smiley' he'll be calling me."

Pam eyed George curiously. "Why, might I ask, are you so flippant about all this? Someone's trying ruin this whole island for us, and you're cracking jokes!"

"*Settle down!* Nobody's gonna ruin nothin' around here. Trust me — all's been looked after."

"Really?!" Pam continued eyeing George. "That sly look on your face — what the heck are you up to, anyway?"

His grin disappearing, George said, "Shhh. Keep your voice down." In a faint whisper he then added, "Just trust me."

By eleven o'clock all guests had arrived and the reunion was in full swing. Just over forty family members of all ages — some standing, some seated — were now scattered in and around Marcy's cottage. Above the din of countless conversations could be heard shrieks, rounds of laughter, and music from the band, which had set up on the front deck. "You've quite a lively bunch here!" Pam half-shouted to a delighted host. Marcy seemingly could not have been more pleased with how the event was unfolding.

Amid all this the islanders continued helping with various tasks at hand. Naturally Roger and Evan were now back on the island and they assumed the chore of producing a barbecue lunch. George, meanwhile, served as bartender while Pam was "cleanup crew," tending to the latest crisis, wherever that might be.

As chance had it for Pam, what she perceived as the greatest crisis took place at her very own patio table, which the Marsdens brought to Marcy's. At that table were initially seated Reed along with Ben and Sheila Ferguson. That situation itself did not bother her, but when she spotted Reed inviting Marcy to join the table she sensed deep trouble brewing. She'd already thought this particular strategy of Reed's through.

Ben and Sheila Ferguson were clearly patriarch and matriarch of the reunion. Ben, much younger brother of Whisper pioneer Gord Ferguson, had recently turned ninety-two, while Sheila was in her mid-eighties. Everyone in attendance, young and old, took turns paying their respects to this venerable couple. Similarly, their respect in return was highly valued — especially by Marcy — and this fact was what, from Pam's perspective, made them dangerous. 'Uncle Ben and Aunt Sheila' could prove a powerful tool for Reed in securing his old cottage. If he could get Marcy to agree to a sale in front of the elderly Ferguson couple, she would thereafter feel utterly obligated to honour that oral agreement. Later denying Reed would make Marcy consider herself 'a complete family disgrace.' Reed therefore didn't require a signature from Marcy to achieve his goal.

Tragically for Pam, the host of the day had her too consumed with chores to even get close enough to eavesdrop, let alone 'contribute' to her patio table's conversation. Frustrated beyond measure, she could only watch, and pray, from afar.

As Marcy took a seat at the table, Reed said brightly, "Here's the girl of the day!"

"Oh go on, you!" Marcy countered, laughing. To Ben and Sheila she said, "Isn't he a sweetheart?"

Sheila said, "He most certainly is. A heartsick person too, it seems."

Marcy's forehead creased. "Sick? You're not feeling well, Reed? Is it the —"

"No, no, Marcy!" said Ben. "We mean he misses something. And the something is this island. Reed was just sharing with us some of his fond memories here."

"Oh yes! Yes, he's done that a lot with me too over the last few years. Seems he regrets selling me the cottage."

Ben said to Reed, "You mentioned earlier, though, that you really didn't have a choice?"

Reed shrugged. "Times were tough back then. I'm comfortable now, though, so ..." He voiced this last word smiling at Marcy.

"Yes, I saw that fancy Cadillac at the landing," said Ben. "That's yours, isn't it? You've done well for yourself, Reed."

"Can't complain."

"Reed even has enough wealth to spread it around a bit," said Marcy. Goofily, she added, "He feels he needs to save me from 'the soup line.'"

"Now, now, Marcy," Reed said softly. "This is not the

time or place for talk about ... problems. Today is about *opportunities*. What I think you should tell Uncle Ben and Aunt Sheila — right now — is the arrangement we've been discussing over the last few years, the one ... you *promised* me. That's what's really important today, dear."

And with that, Reed rose and left the table.

Both Ben's and Sheila's eyes were now, of course, directly on Marcy. There they stayed for almost half a minute, during which time Marcy remained silent. Only a dazed and wavering, nervous smile did she offer.

Eventually Sheila asked, "You ... have something exciting to tell us, Marcy?"

Marcy first swallowed nervously, but then at last her eyes sparkled, and she said, "Why, yes I do. I have a very exciting announcement for both of you."

About an hour later, and just before supper, Pam pulled Evan aside. Standing close to him, she very anxiously said, "Heard anything?"

"A few things. When I delivered a drink to Reed I overheard him say he'll fit right in with the rest of us on the island. Does that mean Marcy's already decided to sell?"

"Better not have. Regarding fitting in, I'd like to fit that scumbag into a box."

"I also heard ... that at supper they'll be making some big announcement."

Pam's heart sunk, and before storming off, she said, "Great — now I'm a *total* basket case."

Like the barbecue lunch, supper was a relatively simple affair. Marcy was determined not to hire a caterer, and so she and Pam planned a dinner they, with help, could produce between their two kitchens. All went well on this front, and about five o'clock Marcy called everyone, including the band, to take seats at three large tables set up in her front yard.

What followed was pure agony for Pam, Roger, and Evan — the longest supper they could remember. On several occasions they even deliberately claimed certain items were 'fresh out' just to speed things up. George, on the other hand, seemed completely relaxed, and Roger was now praying he had some sort of miracle in the works.

The group finished dessert about seven, and it was at this time Ben Ferguson rose and begged everyone's attention. "Please, people — please."

When all had quieted, he said, "I'd like to offer a few words, if I may. First of all, I believe some appreciation for our lovely host is in order."

After hearty applause and numerous cheers, Ben continued with, "I'd also like to recognize my fine nephew, Reed — today's true guest of honour — for proposing this marvellous reunion."

Once again the group cheered.

"And for footing the bill."

Now came laughter amid applause.

When his crowd had once more quieted, Ben said, "Our family, as all of you know, has considerable history on Whisper Island. Our much missed Gord and Nora, along with Reed, cherished this island, rough as it may seem, for countless years. Since their departure dear Marcy has held the torch, and she too has accumulated many joyous memories here. It thus strikes me as very fitting that our family's presence on Whisper continue, and continue strong."

A hush now fell over the group, and it became obvious rumours of a special announcement had circulated.

After devilishly allowing suspense to build a moment, Ben smiled especially warmly and delivered, "That said, I'm pleased to announce the engagement of our beloved Marcy to someone whom I'm sure you've all by now met — Mr. George Clarke."

"Why didn't you just tell us?! You liked seeing us suffer?"

This came from Pam, who had only recently recovered from shock.

"Sorry — Marcy made me swear to secrecy," George apologetically explained. "She wanted it to be a big secret for today." George grinned before adding, "Especially for Reed, of course."

"I do believe you achieved the desired effect," Roger said with a chortle. "Poor guy seems to have a glaze over his eyes."

Pam said, "I almost died when I overheard Marcy say to him, 'Isn't it fantastic, Reed? Now you don't have to worry about me and my money problems anymore. I'm looked after!' Pam laughed. "I absolutely loved that!"

Evan said, "Where is Reed now?"

"Who knows? Probably sulking somewhere. Why?"

Mr. Dean smirked. "Because I wanted to see him sulking. I have this dreamlike image in my head, but I'd like to see the real thing."

Pam said, "I don't doubt you're getting images, boy, the way you've been pushing back the beverages the last hour."

"Hey!" Evan said with shaky glass high. "Can you blame a slob for celebratin' the won'ers of love?" With that he rejoined (stumbled back into) the crowd with Roger.

Now alone with George, Pam beamed a huge smile at him. "You big ... teddy bear, lady's man, love muffin, you!" She followed this with a hug, or at least attempted to. "You *finally* broke down, and your timing couldn't have been better. This is perfect, absolutely *perfect*." Albeit awkwardly, Pam now treated herself to several hops about the grass.

Watching, George said, "You wouldn't be seeing a few things yourself right now, would you, Pammy?"

"Haven't had a drop."

"Liar."

"There's only one liar here today, and you fixed him, Georgie 'Don Juan' Clarke. You fixed him, lover-boy!"

Georgie sighed. "You're a pain."

Since most had lengthy drives home, Marcy's guests began departing about 9:00 p.m. Not surprisingly, Reed Ferguson was among them.

"Not staying until Sunday night now, Reed?" Roger asked from his boat while docked at Marcy's. He didn't expect an answer, and he didn't get one.

Reed also wasn't especially chatty when Roger later delivered him to the mainland. This after the captain had taken every other guest; Roger insisted on saving the "guest of honour" for a "special trip." Marcy's cousin did at last speak up, though, when he reached his car.

Seemed it wouldn't start.

While Reed had himself a nasty cursing fit, Roger did likewise. "Wouldn't you bloody well know it?" he snarled, pounding the Cadillac's hood with his fist almost hard enough to dent it. "Not even for a *family reunion* will these bloody vandals lay off! Can you *believe* these punks?"

"Sure, whatever," said Reed, fuming. "So how about driving me to Kirkdale's? I don't have all night."

"'Fraid I didn't bring my car keys, partner. And besides, the mechanic won't be around the place right now. Tell you what, though — when I get back to the island I'll call Arnold Knapp at home. I'm sure he'll come running."

"I'd rather you just called a tow —"

"No, no! You sit tight. Good old reliable Arnie will be here to save you." Turning toward his boat, Roger said to himself, "In a couple of hours, that is — when I tell him to undo his handiwork."

16

"It's like someone's switched the bloomin' sun back on!" was how Pam Marsden described her mood following Marcy's fateful reunion. The others surely would have agreed; with Reed and his hired gun now out of the picture it seemed cottage life for all would return to its normal, pleasant self. Pam was, however, the architect of an event to officially celebrate the end to the islanders' torment. On the Wednesday following Marcy's reunion she decided Evan would host a small but rather lively party ("he has the best stereo, after all"). Such gatherings were easy to bring about on Green Heron — a few words distributed at Kirkdale's sufficed — and the evening went over well. Indeed Pam's last and fondest memory was of being carried home by a laughing and staggering George and Evan.

Mostly, though, the islanders celebrated Whisper's brightened atmosphere by merely indulging in their favourite quiet pastimes. Marcy spent hours at a time fussing over her gardens, George dreamt up all manner of 'critically important' projects at her place, and Evan made sure his lounge chair was sufficiently weighted down. Pam, meanwhile, indulged in several early morning 'runs.' "Twelve laps and not even winded!" she once offered to a puzzled Roger upon return.

On the final Thursday of August, and the final Thursday of their holidays, the islanders gathered at the Marsdens in typical fashion for a 'sunsetter.' Evan of all souls took command on this particular occasion, providing "the grub," which consisted of hamburgers done on the barbecue. While he set to work, and while Marcy fixed a salad inside, Pam, Roger, and George held sway over the deck chairs.

Roger raised the first issue of discussion on this warm, clear evening. He was deeply concerned. Ever since the islanders began taking their holidays together he had proposed certain "rules of cottage vacation behaviour," and to these his neighbours unanimously agreed. But one such rule, "Thou shalt not returneth to the city during thy holidays," was apparently about to be broken.

It seemed, however, the sinner had no choice.

"Bernie next door to me said probably most of a bundle of shingles have come off a back section of my roof," George apologetically explained to Roger. "I've heard we're getting rain this coming Sunday, so I figure I better get on it."

Roger absorbed this presentation, then countered with, "Can't con Bernie into looking after it? You've done enough favours for him over the years, haven't you?"

George shook his head vigorously. "The old duffer's not up to anything like that. Nope, I'll have to whip down, Rog. Sorry."

Pam asked, "Did Bernie have any theories why you suddenly lost some shingles?"

"He figures a strong wind did it, and he's probably right. The shingles are old and curled up on the ends. I'm due to replace the whole lot."

First making sure Marcy remained out of earshot, Roger quietly said, "You're confident some other ... *force* in the universe didn't cause the problem?"

"I am. Wouldn't put it past that force, but I don't think so in this case. I've just got an old roof."

To Pam, Roger said, "While we're on this unfortunate topic, has Marcy mentioned anything about her wonderful cousin since the reunion? Do you know if he's called her?"

Pam shrugged. "She's never mentioned anything about him calling. She *has* said several times 'it's so wonderful Reed isn't worrying about me anymore.' I almost barf when I hear that."

"I'd rather hear her saying that than 'Reed ran a new idea past me.'"

"I don't feel we have to worry anymore — he was soundly defeated." Turning to George, Pam added, "Thanks to our Casanova here." To this she received a predictable grimace.

Marcy now returned from the kitchen with a salad bowl cradled in her hands. Pam said to her, "Marcy! We were talking about the wedding plans. When I suggested a hundred guests George scoffed. He said we're having no fewer than two hundred to the island."

Marcy's eyes lit up. "Two hun—!"

"Now don't go givin' her ideas!" George broke in, sighing heavily.

"I'm thinking several cakes, too," Pam continued undaunted. "And a slew of antique boats to parade around the lake."

"Sounds pretty nice, Georgie," Roger mischievously threw in, grinning at his neighbour.

Fighting to remain calm, George quietly offered to Pam and Marcy, "We'll just have a nice little simple ... *thing*, I figure, out on the headland or somewhere. Is that mushy enough for you two?"

Pam smiled. "You're not foolin' me, you big softy. Heck,

I bet you've even booked a little orchestra, haven't you?"

George put his hands on his face. "Oh, Lord."

Conversation continued on other fronts the remainder of this evening, only pausing when the sun put on its final show about eight. On this day it was particularly dazzling — the low, western horizon bathed in orange and crimson red as the golden sun slowly dipped behind the trees of the mainland. Or perhaps, as Pam later wondered, maybe it was their mood making it so special. She was a firm believer in 'You often don't truly appreciate something until you lose it,' and clearly all knew they'd almost lost sunsetters at Whisper.

Roger was so touched, but not for long. Shortly after biting into a final hamburger Evan courteously delivered, the frog tucked under the bun decided 'enough was enough' and proceeded to squirm out and hop lakeward. What followed was Evan all but falling over in laughter, and Roger soon after chasing him halfway around the island. "I didn't tell you, Evan — he prefers frogs in his *salad*!" Pam yelled. So ended the evening's festivities.

Unfortunately for the islanders of Whisper, the jovial atmosphere of that evening proved short-lived.

George arrived back at the lake about five-thirty on Saturday. He was not long in loading his boat with a duffle bag of clothes and a cooler of groceries. He was therefore also not long in discovering his outboard motor had been tampered with.

This situation did not come to him as a surprise. Turned out, the wind didn't blow the shingles off his city roof. He considered it a nice try by Reed, but unfortunately he opted to use a spade, and George spotted the tell-tale marks on the shingles. With this revelation, he journeyed back to Whisper on this day both cranky and fully expecting more "little tidbits of revenge."

Luckily, he had a spare motor stored in his cargo trailer. Like his 'good' motor, she was also an oldie and hurting, but would do for the weekend. Nonetheless, he cursed under his breath at Reed several times. "How pathetic can you get?"

The spare motor was unfortunately buried at the back of the trailer behind a mound of items, including his ancient snowmobile. But not wanting to give Reed the satisfaction of this proving a major hindrance, George quickly negotiated his way to the trailer's rear wall. And perhaps being so determined was why he didn't notice the trailer doors swinging closed behind him until they were completely shut.

At first he thought a gust of wind was responsible. But then he heard the click of the padlock.

"Hey!" he shouted, viciously plowing his way from the back of the trailer to the door. Pounding hard, he roared, "You're in a bloody heap of trouble with this, Ferguson!"

His threats, however, did not seem to deter his captor. Shortly after, George heard a distant and peculiar skidding sound, then a few minutes later the creak of his hitch crank. Very soon after that, he fell over as the trailer lurched forward.

17

About six-thirty that same Saturday evening, an hour after George reached Ferg Landing, the Marsdens received a call. It was Marcy.

"Have you seen George?"

"Not yet, dear," Pam answered. "You were expecting him at a certain time?"

"Six o'clock. I had dinner ready a half hour ago. A very nice dinner, if I may say so."

"I'm afraid we haven't heard anything. I wouldn't worry too much, though, Marcy. This is the Labour Day weekend — it's entirely possible he's tied up in traffic on the highway. Have you tried him in the city yet?"

"Yes I did. There was no answer."

"Then almost for sure he's in a traffic jam. You'll just have to hold tight."

About an hour and a half after that call, at dusk, Roger walked to George's cottage to return an axe and other assorted tools. He'd earlier received a report from Pam about Marcy's concerns but only assumed his neighbour had since arrived. It wasn't until reaching George's shed and casually glancing out to shore that Roger himself became concerned: *The Pride of Whisper* was not at the dock.

Supposing George may have tied up at Marcy's, but

wanting to be sure, Roger immediately headed to the island's southeastern point. When he arrived he found an obviously distressed Marcy standing on her front deck, arms tightly folded, speaking with Evan.

Her dock was empty, but Roger nonetheless said, "He's still not here?"

With a quaver to her voice, Marcy answered, "No, and he hasn't called, and no one has seen him. I've phoned umpteen friends on the mainland. I finally rang up Pam again a minute ago — she's now headed here. My goodness, though! I do hope I'm not annoying people."

Roger said, "Don't be silly."

"You call us at any time of the day for any reason," added Pam, now approaching along shore. When she reached the deck she said, "Very sorry for not following up on George, Marcy, but I'm afraid I nodded off after supper. I can't believe he *still* isn't here."

Turning and eyeing her, Roger said, "I don't think we should ring the alarm bells too loud just yet, though."

Taking this cue, Pam adopted a more relaxed and soothing voice. "Yes, I suppose you're right. It *is* the Labour Day weekend, after all — delays and setbacks are to be expected." Standing behind Marcy and rubbing her arms, Pam added, "I'm sure everything's fine. And if you're nice supper is ruined I'll help you make a new one."

"Tell you what," Roger said. "Evan and I will run over to the landing. Could be George's old boat simply won't start and he's caught up in trying to fix it. I know myself how the hours can slip away in a flash with something like that."

Marcy said, "I would really appreciate the trip. Are you sure you don't mind going along, Evan?"

"No, I'll go, Marcy. I'll help."

"Then let's head out," said Roger, glancing severely at

Evan and beckoning him to immediately follow. Facing his own cottage as he spoke, Roger said to the girls, "Who knows how long we'll be — don't get uptight if we aren't back for an hour or more." With that he and Evan continued along shore.

When they reached the Marsdens' dock Evan asked, "Why'd you give me that look back there?"

Pausing a second from untying his boat, Roger answered, "Because I've got a bad feeling something's going on, Ev."

They utilized all available horsepower getting to the landing. Upon seeing *The Pride* still docked there, Roger suggested they head straight for Kirkdale's. He knew the store was closed but out of habit newly-arrived cottagers often still briefly stopped there.

His prediction proved accurate. When they reached Kirkdale's in Roger's car they came upon an elderly couple driving a pickup with a fifth wheel trailer attached. A curly-haired woman in denim jeans and jacket was presently using the store's phone booth. Roger and Evan briefly spoke with the driver, who remained in the truck.

"The highway was pretty good, actually," the stocky, gray-haired man said. "I saw a few vehicles conked out, though, and I've seen a few pass in the time we've been sitting here. What's your buddy driving?"

Roger said, "A chocolate brown Ford pickup. Vintage."

The man mused a second, then said, "Nope, can't say I've seen anything like that. Sorry."

Roger next tried knocking on the Kirkdales' apartment door but received no answer. Ten minutes of hanging around the store's parking lot, and questioning several more passing cottagers, also yielded no information.

Back on the road neither Roger nor Evan knew where else specifically to look, so they drove about randomly the next hour. With no progress made, Roger suggested they check back at the landing.

When they found George's boat still there they both searched with flashlights for clues he'd at least been at the landing at one point that evening. It was then Evan noticed something missing.

Shining his flashlight on the spot where George's cargo trailer should have been, he said, "Did George take his trailer with him when he left for the city?"

"He didn't mention about doing that," said Roger. "I suppose it's possible he decided to at the last min—"

Roger broke off, because Evan was now shining his flashlight at several long skid marks, right where George normally parked his truck. "He *was* here," said Evan. "Looks like he showed up in a hurry, too. That's a mean skid."

"Wait a minute," said Roger, shining his own flashlight farther along the gravel parking lot. "There's no bloody way he skidded *that* far."

The skid marks stretched seemingly forever. Indeed, quickly tracing them Roger and Evan wound up at the Burkes' vacant cottage, some fifty yards from the landing. Sitting in the cottage's laneway, sure enough, was George's truck.

Mesmerized, Evan said, "Somebody *dragged it* all the way over here!?"

For a moment Roger could only stare. At last he said, "This is not good. Not good at all."

Howard Kirkdale had looked forward to the trip the entire week. She'd been warm, and "extremely soon" after closing the store on Saturday evening he and Arnold Knapp took off for their treasured Partridge Lake. And to rescue their week the fishing proved terrific.

Nearing ten o'clock both yawned contentedly as they loaded Howard's bass boat onto his trailer. The boss was still awake enough, however, that once negotiating the lake's overgrown access road he noticed something new.

Suddenly pointing right he said to his mechanic, "Now who in God's gracious name stuck *that* there tonight?"

The cargo trailer had been backed snugly into a patch of thick alders, but not so far that when Howard pulled right and stopped he didn't recognize the unit in his headlights. He, after all, had sold it to its present owner.

Some ten minutes worth of cursing and lock-smashing later that owner sat in Howard's cab with all but steam hissing from his ears. "Warp frickin' speed to the cop station!" he roared, wiping his sweaty, beet-red face. Even with boat in tow the driver could only obey.

They were on the main road about ten minutes when George, just slightly calmed, spat out, "So *neither* of you recognized the tire marks in front of the trailer?!"

Arnold shrugged, albeit very nervously. "Sure I know the tires, George, but lots of guys around Green Heron have those on their trucks."

George eyed Arnold harshly. "What about Reed Ferguson?"

Before Arnold could answer, Howard said, "Don't think

so. He stopped by the garage earlier this summer and I noticed he was driving a DeVille. Mind, I suppose with his money he could have a truck as well."

"Damn right the bloody swindler could," George blared. "In fact — now I *know* so."

Innocently, Howard said, "But ... surely you don't feel *Reed Ferguson* is responsible for this, do you? The son of our beloved Gord and Nora?"

Glancing again at Arnold, who by now was rubbing flipper-sized boots together in familiar fashion, George answered, "I won't go into why, Howard, but it's a little more than a feeling."

Howard said, "I can help you with this, then — Rose saw him earlier today when she was out in the car."

"Well there you go. And was he in a pickup?"

"That I don't know. I also don't know where exactly she saw him — you'd have to talk to her."

After viciously spitting out his window, George said, "Then kindly get me to Rose, dear Howard."

When reaching Kirkdale's some twenty minutes later they nearly ran over Roger and Evan. The two were headed across the dark gravel parking lot, toward Roger's car, when the rapidly oncoming freight train almost tagged them.

George had his door open and was out before Howard even got the truck and trailer completely stopped.

"What in blazes is going on?!" Roger immediately barked. George followed with a quick and heated account of his recent setback, ending with his present mission.

Now equally fired up, Roger said, "I don't know where the heck Rose *is*, though, George. We've just finished banging on the Kirkdales' door for the second time tonight. She must have gone out."

"Naw. Don't worry — she's home," said Howard, beckoning the others to follow. "She's got some girls over playing euchre tonight, and they probably didn't hear you knocking. That or they tried damn hard not to hear — naturally we avoid answering after we've closed for the day."

While the islanders waited outside the Kirkdales' lamp-lit door, Howard went upstairs to get Rose. The Whisper crew chose to wait, of course, because they gained the opportunity to privately interrogate someone in their midst.

Looking like he very much desired to be elsewhere, Arnold Knapp soon had a meaty finger pointed in his face courtesy of George. "You need to start talkin' mister. Lord help you if I find out you knew Reed was around tonight."

Holding both hands in the air, Arnold anxiously pleaded, "I swear I didn't, George. I absolutely swear. Howard didn't say nothin' to me in the boat about Rose seeing Reed today. I also haven' seen or talked to Reed in over a month. Not since you boys —"

"Pulled you out from under an outhouse?" This question Evan delivered, and he was answered with a sneer.

Roger said, "So for the record — you're saying you knew nothing about anyone planning a number on George tonight?"

"Didn' know a thing," said Arnold, putting a hand to his heart. "I also wouldna done this mysel—"

"Don't feed me *that*!" Roger fired back. "Because of your little fishing trip we know you didn't relocate George, but don't tell me you *wouldn't* have done it. Give me a friggin' break!"

In Arnold's face again, George added, "You realize we can turn you in to Howard and the cops anytime — right? You *do* realize that?"

Head down, Arnold nodded.

"Then you'd bloody well better be straight with us. You'd also better dream up a way of making yourself useful. For example, I'm thinkin' you at least have some idea where our fine friend might be right now."

Arnold only shook his head, but before George could press harder the Kirkdales' door opened. Dressed elegantly in heels and a flower-print dress, a perfumed Rose stepped out, Howard in tow.

"I saw Reed over by Brandon Point," she immediately reported. "He was in his Cadillac, though, so I don't know if he's your man."

"When was this?" George politely asked.

"About four this afternoon."

"Was he pulling out of someone's cottage?"

"No. Just parked at the side of the road talking."

Roger asked, "Did you happen to see who with?"

"Not really. But I recognized the truck parked in front of Reed's car. It was Stan Milne's. Does that mean anything?"

At the sound of the name George all but did a back flip. Only Roger was calm enough to say, "Holy friggin' cow — maybe the bugger was in on Reed's whole scheme after all."

"I swear, Rog," George snarled, now pacing with fists clenched. "I swear, when I find that bas—"

Looking utterly confused, Rose cut in with, "But ... why on earth would Stan be mixed up in your problems?"

"Because Stan is Stan," George answered matter-of-factly. Quickly turning, he said to Howard, "Know if *Stan's* tires match the tracks back at the trailer?"

The storekeeper nodded gravely. "Put 'em on myself."

George turned again to Roger. "No way I'm wrong this time. No bloody way. Stan's in on it, meaning we're now hunting two guys —"

He cut this declaration short, because at this moment a green Buick roared into the parking lot.

"Oh, that's Tom Burke all ticked off," said George. "I forgot — you said my truck's now blocking their laneway. Apparently they just arrived from the city."

When the car skidded to a stop beside the group, George immediately said, "Real, real sorry, Tommy. I'll head over right away and move the truck."

Coughing through the gravel dust he'd stirred up, Tom managed to say, "Not here about that. You boys need to get home — pronto!"

Roger said, "What's going on?"

Amid more coughing, Tom croaked, "George's cottage is on fire."

18

Through the darkness they naturally saw the fire long before reaching it. Once at Ferg Landing, George could see tiny flickers of bright orange at the island's northern end. "I don't think it's all that well established yet," he blared while frantically untying a line on Roger's boat. "We've got a shot."

A fire was any islander's worst fear on Green Heron. With no fire boat available cottagers are left to volunteer fire fighters arriving in their own boats, and to their own devices. Most invest in a portable fire pump and this was fortunately true of all the islanders on Whisper. Nonetheless, fighting a fire with such meagre equipment and experience was a daunting task.

Several of the island's four pumps were already in use when the men arrived in Roger's boat and Tom Burke's. Four mainlanders were currently battling the fire, which proved more substantial than George had thought. The cottage's northwestern corner, home to the living room, was entirely engulfed in flames.

In hysterics, Pam charged awkwardly toward the dock as the boats came in, almost tumbling into the lake when she reached them. "I really don't know how long ago it started or how," she reported through sobs and while wiping tears.

"I'm so sorry, George."

Evan led in reaching the cottage, having leapt out even before Roger's boat touched the dock. George, Roger, Tom Burke, Howard Kirkdale, and Arnold Knapp followed soon after.

"Where's Marcy?" George immediately asked Pam, scanning the yard. "Is she at her place?"

Pam nodded. "She's on the phone calling for more help. We need it; the guys have only George's and our pump going so far. Someone needs to get the others — they're too heavy for me."

"Arnold and I will grab them," Howard quickly offered, motioning to Evan to provide his shed key.

As Howard and Arnold raced off in the Marsdens' boat to fetch the pumps, George and Roger took stock of the situation. As hard as the mainlanders were working, the fire was slowly but surely spreading. With the heat and smoke keeping them at bay they were having great difficulty distributing water inside the building. Even with George's large front window now smashed some areas of the cottage's interior were burning unhindered.

"This is not doing it," George yelled. "I'm gonna have a crack at fighting it from inside."

"No!" Roger shouted back. "That's crazy — way too dangerous!"

Knowing this was true, but adrenaline pushing him forward anyway, within several minutes George entered the cottage through the south end side door, dragging an idle fire hose. "Let 'er rip," he yelled when he was in position. Seconds later lake water blasted from the hose and George had to keep a very tight hold. Immediately he began spraying at those areas the mainland cottagers were unable to reach from outside. These included the rafters, which George could access after Roger, who suddenly appeared at his side, started tearing down ceiling tiles with a shovel.

Later reflecting on these efforts, George supposed if they'd begun this interior battle even fifteen minutes earlier they might well have won. As it was, the fire had simply progressed too far. When their eyes stung so badly from the smoke they couldn't see, and the heat became too intense, they were forced to retreat.

Once back outside, coughing and rubbing their eyes, they were in poor shape to stop Evan. He figured fresh eyes and lungs were simply needed, and proceeded to take up the hose. Right before he entered the cottage, however, a large and unyielding arm stopped him.

"Don't you dare," George said. "Just leave it — the place is gone, Ev."

When he had somewhat recovered George had the two fire hoses directed at the surrounding forest. Especially so 'General Whisper,' the island's giant pine. Amid this change of strategy Howard arrived back in Roger's boat with the other two fire pumps. This, at least, was what everyone thought he had.

As Howard rapidly approached from the dock, George filled him in. "We've given up on the cottage. We're now just drenching the bush so it doesn't end up on fire."

"But that's why I'm back without Arnold or the pumps," Howard said, puffing heavily. "On the other side of the island, the bush already *is* on fire."

The following two hours became a blur of frantic activity

for all on Whisper Island this night. 'All' soon numbered many; Marcy's frenetic phone calling paid off, and by 1:30 a.m nearly a hundred souls were on the island, including police. This force divided its efforts between containing the fire at George's place, and containing that threatening the forest on the island's eastern shore, some three hundred yards north of the Dean cottage. The bush fire Howard Kirkdale fortunately spotted in its infancy, so with the pumps of many cottagers soon at work it was reasonably controlled. As well, shortly after 1:30 a.m something else happened to further limit the fires: it began to rain.

"Thank heavens!" Marcy screeched from Evan's front deck when this precipitation commenced, and her cry was seconded by many. The forecasted rain George had worried about concerning his roof in Whitby had come.

As it increased in tempo, many of those fighting the fires finally had a chance to take a break. Among these were a very fatigued George and Roger. Both were sweating profusely and were covered from head to toe in soot and ash. With her storied garden hose Pam sprayed each off in turn.

It was soon after Roger received a cup of coffee in Evan's kitchen that a police officer approached him. "Mr. Marsden?"

"Yes?"

"We need you and George Clarke to come with us to the mainland right away."

"What's up?"

"We got a call — we believe a cruiser just stopped Reed Ferguson on the highway."

"You *believe* it's him?" Roger soon inquired as he, George, and several police officers boated to Ferg Landing.

One officer said, "He claims to have no identification —

says he forgot his wallet at home. What he did have with him, though, was a Cadillac DeVille and an awfully nervous face."

"Gonna be even more nervous pretty soon," said George.

The police had pulled their suspect over just north of Peterborough, meaning the islanders faced an hour's drive. When they at last arrived at the station, however, they needed only about another three seconds to I.D. one Reed Ferguson.

"Screw you," was the first thing he said to George and Roger. Then came, "Screw the bunch of you."

So began a round of interrogation that ended with Reed essentially admitting to his crimes. This after a slip up regarding his whereabouts the evening of the previous day. Seems at one point he was at home in Toronto and the next minute he was visiting Marcy on Whisper. It all went downhill for him from there, and at last he came out with "It's *my* island, and I'd rather see it burnt to the ground than in your hands!" That effectively sealed the evening.

As he and George were leaving, Roger said to Reed, now in handcuffs, "Your parents would be horrified if they could see you now. They were good community people. Lord knows what happened to you."

To this came a predictable, "I forgot — screw them too."

Despite their hellish night, that morning the sun still rose on schedule on Whisper Island. It did so, however, to mostly ashes at the Clarke lot, and to its owner wearily sifting through them with a half-charred shovel.

"At least I won't be working again on that blessed foundation," George said with chin up to Pam and Roger, who had recently joined him.

"Exactly — now you can make a total disaster of a brand new foundation," Roger softly jabbed. "Or is that the plan?"

George answered, "Nope — the wife says she's taking me in."

"'The wife', huh?" Pam said with a smile. "Didn't think she'd graduated to such a lofty status yet."

"Suppose things are headed that way soon enough, though, aren't they?"

Pam quipped, "Just as soon as we make a special trip to the city for napkins, Mr. Clarke."

By now all who had helped fight the fires had returned home, and aside from conversation on the island's northwestern corner, a peaceful quiet had again settled over Whisper. Evan and Marcy, both exhausted, were presently sound asleep in their respective cottages, and George and the Marsdens would soon follow in their footsteps.

In the meantime, Pam said to her fellow islanders, "It's a wonder anyone could become so deranged that they'd do something like this. It's a crazy world."

"No, it's only a crazy Reed, I think," said George. "A completely self-centered guy who got way, way too bitter about something and then lost control of himself. I won't be taking this out on the whole world."

Pam said, "And that guy is gone for good now?"

"Well, he's in jail. What more can we do?"

"Hope he never gets out," answered Pam. "And what about his pal — he's not in jail. Think Stan Milne will ever get nailed for any of this?"

George shook his head. "Somehow doubt it. I think if the cops had enough to lay charges on him they'd have done it by now. No, the slippery scoundrel will get off, I'm afraid."

Roger said, "One thing I've connected on this morning is that he was Reed's little informant. Someone had to tell Reed the police weren't making trips to the island anymore to investigate vandalism. He clearly knew we'd caught Arnold. Looks like that informant was Stan."

"Oh, sure," said George. "Those two apparently go way back. Tom Burke told me last night Stan was a long-time client of Reed's. They were close friends."

Roger said, "Okay, so that brings me to a puzzle: if Stan wanted a place on this island bad enough to kidnap you and play a hand in maybe more, why didn't he simply buy the Willett's cottage from Reed when he was selling?"

"My guess is because Reed knew he could get a lot more money out of Marcy," said George. "I'm sure Reed didn't tell Stan that; probably said he sold it to Marcy to 'keep the place in the family.' But I figure money was the real issue. Isn't that a swell way to be with a close friend?"

"Simply stupendous," said Pam, mimicking Marcy's voice. Soon she added, "So we still have Stan to worry about, then?".

"I don't think he'd dare try anything more now that Reed's caught," said Roger. "But as George said, it's not likely he'll ever be brought to justice."

"I feel so bad for Mary Milne," said Pam. "She's so nice."

George said, "Well, don't feel *too* awful — Mary at least won't be climbing up and down those stairs at her place anymore."

Almost in unison, Pam and Roger said, "Why's that?"

"I called Stan this morning and told him my lot was now

for sale. He made me a good offer right on the spot."

After delivering this announcement George held a straight face an impressive five seconds.

"You bloody bugger!" Pam finally said, tossing a charred piece of lumber at George as he laughed and strode away toward Marcy's place.

As he did so, however, he at last put in his pocket a small, ash-dusted metal plate he'd been secretly holding all this time — one on which 'Whispered Greetings' was still clearly discernible.

19

Like most lakes in Ontario's cottage country Green Heron is quiet after Labour Day, especially so on weekdays. School resumes and by now most in the workforce have taken their holidays. Yet some, mainly retirees, do continue cottaging and in fact prefer the autumn months. Indeed with much quieter lakes and cooler weather many contend the day after Labour Day "is when the cottage season truly begins."

Stan and Mary Milne were among those dubbed "fall types." Rarely were they absent at Green Heron during autumn. Often the couple was spotted still boating to Franklin Island when the lake was partly ice-covered; seemingly nothing could hold them back.

Such was certainly true the autumn of 2002. Despite Mary falling on the steep path to their dock in late summer and badly fracturing her right leg, the Milnes remained on Green Heron. And they were rewarded; weather was mostly splendid this year.

On a rare contrary day in mid-September Stan rose just after dawn and thus ahead of Mary. Silently slipping from bed he padded to the kitchen for a quick coffee, then as quickly dressed in the spare room and stepped out into the morning, which was cool and misty.

For the last several weeks he had been slowly and

painfully constructing a lakeside gazebo — Mary's grand idea
for this fine-weathered autumn — and before finishing he
had depleted his lumber supply. But Stan decided that
wouldn't be a problem. He was aware of a cottage being built
on the mainland, and was also aware, via eavesdropping on a
silly new employee at Kirkdale's, the crew wouldn't be
working this Wednesday. Therefore, lots of lumber lying
unattended.

When he'd descended to the dock he untied his pontoon
boat but didn't start the motor. To avoid waking Mary he
would first paddle a short distance. With luck he'd return
before she rose, and thus escape questions about where one
buys lumber on Green Heron just after dawn.

Seated at the edge of the boat's carpeted deck he paddled
only some twenty feet before pausing.

Initially he tried calming himself by raffling off in his
head all manner of possibilities. Perhaps, for instance, the
hooks holding their 'Milne Cottage' sign, which hung from a
nearby L-shaped post, had become rusted. Alas, there was no
breeze this morning to make the sign swing. He also noted,
to his very anxious chagrin, the creaking sounds were
increasing in volume, and were familiar — sounds that had
endlessly rung in his ears over a year of absence on Green
Heron.

Stan Milne did not share with a single soul — not even
Mary — what he saw come out of the lake mist that
morning. There would be no distributing a photograph this
time. He did not, considering his intended mission, even
mention to anyone he was out that early. As such, Mary and
neighbouring cottagers found it puzzling, considering the
fortunate weather and the Milnes' love of autumn, he would
insist on leaving the island later that day. Downright

baffling, however, was Stan soon insisting they sell the cottage, and his accepting several bars shy of a song two weeks later.

Naturally rumours soon abounded concerning what caused the Milnes' sudden departure from the lake. Had someone said something to irreparably offend them? Was the couple having marital problems? Were they hurting financially? It became quite an issue on the lake.

Such was the main topic of conversation on Whisper Island the first Saturday of October. George, amid borrowing assorted tools from Evan's shed, ran into its owner when he and Howard Kirkdale dropped in for coffee. Also taking advantage of the good weather, Howard had left the store in Rose's hands and was putting in a full day retiring boats for the winter. This in the company of his new right-hand man.

Stan and Mary Milne were not the only long-time residents on Green Heron now absent. Immediately after the Labour Day weekend, citing "stress — way, way too much stress," Arnold Knapp moved on to other mechanical pastures. This had left Roger Marsden snickering but Howard Kirkdale in an unexpected predicament: he could wait until spring to hire another mechanic for the garage, but he needed help immediately for lifting boats. Spotting the job posting on the store's bulletin board, Evan quickly offered his services. And although quite familiar with this particular applicant's reputation, a desperate Howard took a chance and hired him as a full-time employee. As it turned out, Evan fared surprisingly well with the new job; on the lake he provided a strong back and in the store he proved helpful and pleasant with customers — even, notably, with a certain patron he didn't care for. At the store in late September Howard had told George Clarke as much. "It's funny. Either aging or something else has settled the boy down a fair chunk."

Predictably, George wound up having coffee with Evan and Howard that Saturday morning when they stopped in at the Dean cottage. Also predictable was their topic of conversation.

"Darned if I know what happened," Howard said to George with a sigh, soon after they were seated at Evan's kitchen table. "The bugger owes me money, too. Probably never see it now."

"Probably not. And you'd think a buddy would at least stop in to say goodbye and let us wish him Godspeed." George wiped an invisible tear. "Golly gosh darn it upsets me he's gone."

Howard grinned. "Yes. You two had quite a history, didn't you?"

George winked at Evan, who was also now grinning. "You, Howard, have no idea."

"But all tears wiped aside and your nose blown, you must admit it was strange how quickly he jumped ship. He and Mary were on this lake darn near as long as Rose and myself."

After draining his coffee, George offered, "Lord only knows, Howard. I heard through the grapevine Mary Milne is absolutely beside herself over the whole thing. So I figure it's pretty safe to say leaving wasn't her idea."

"Concluded the same," said Howard. Turning to his right-hand man, he asked, "You have any input on this, Mr. Talkative?"

Evan shrugged. "Can't say I do ... really. At the store I hear lots of talk but I can't sort it all out."

George pondered this, studying Evan a moment, then said, "Well, I don't think we should be losing sleep over it all.

Stan's off the lake and that's that. In my humble opinion we should focus now on a more important issue."

Howard's eyebrows rose. "Really? And what's that?"

Prompting considerable laughter, George delivered, "How to *keep* him off the lake."

The three men soon parted that day. Howard and Evan left in their work boat to continue lifting, leaving George at the dock. The latter paused before heading home, wanting to look over again something Evan had recently acquired. The young islander cleverly accepted it from Howard in lieu of pay for his first week.

Amid his study he pulled something else from his pocket: one of Marcy's older wigs — one he had, curiously, found in Evan's shed while rooting for tools.

And one, also curiously, spray-painted wine red.

Contemplating the wig, Evan's aged but newly-acquired tin boat, and the mental image of a peculiar kitchen table gaze, a decidedly devilish smile formed on George Clarke's face this fine, sunny morning.

After playfully tapping the boat's gunnel with his work boot, he turned and started home, electing to put the wig back in his pocket rather than back in the shed. Heck, so nicely painted was it Marcy might even give it a whirl.

20

The sun rises curiously over Whisper Island. The early light caresses it much like a child caressing a stray and bedraggled dog; it is a light sympathetic, and nurturing. Low and unhindered by a thick forest canopy it slips through tangled undergrowth, freshening the island's moist, heavy-aired interior. Along shore, wildflowers declared weeds by cruising boaters now dapple forest edges with glowing whites, purples, and oranges, while nuisance boulders assume a silvery sheen. Similarly the light streams through windows of modest island cottages, warming their interiors and heralding a cherished day for those sleeping within.

It is in such a light, and perhaps only fittingly, a certain nocturnal resident makes a final island tour before retiring. He does so under a title and with a distinction his predecessors have maintained since the beginning of significant time.

On a Saturday morning in September of 2002, that resident began his tour padding slowly but surely along the island's eastern shore. As had been the case for weeks now, he was not impressed. Here fully an acre of his domain had been desecrated; everywhere lay the charred remains of maples, birches, and spruces, and shoreline rocks and gravel were coated in thick, black ash.

So too did he again note destruction on the island's western shore, which he soon reached upon traversing a temporarily breezeless headland. Once home to the 'great snoring brute,' that realm also now lay in ruins. Only a dock remained, and perhaps this too would soon be gone.

But the island's chief resident did not entirely despair. Journeying south he noted Whisper's giant white pine still stood strong and proud. Farther along, a tiny cove remained bursting with singing goldfinches, and nearby, a pair of mergansers dabbled leisurely in the still shaded western shallows.

Yes, he decided, his minions would indeed recover and live on.

He approached cautiously when reaching the island's southwestern point. In past one inhabitant had several times joined him in his official tour. On both occasions she rudely disturbed it with a short and foolish sprint, an unworthy companion to his gallantly reserved stride. On this day he saw no immediate sign of more such annoyances, however, and soon gained further reassurance. Nobly ascending vine-clad latticework, then hopping royally to a nearby window planter, his majesty earned a view within. Bathed in sunlight, both the transgressor and her concierge remained in their treasured burrow, peacefully and seemingly gratefully.

The 'great snoring brute' had merely moved, he knew. Upon reaching the island's eastern point, and while indulging in delicacies left by a flowery angel, he again heard the familiar rumblings through an open screened window. Apparently the coarse creature was here to stay, and, conveniently, under an angel's watchful eye.

A final point of inspection brought continued good news. Now midway along the island's eastern shore, he had, in past, always found this particular burrow one of great turmoil and danger. Seemingly it reflected the 'nature of the beast' residing within. But in recent times, including this day, all was calm, and his highness now even dared to wander through and explore this formerly beleaguered estate.

His tour complete, he now journeyed inland, tracing a path through a still sparse mat of crisp autumn leaves. He would retire to a place unknown to those of the two-legged sort, but used by countless generations of his own.

The entrance to the island's royal burrow was, at it should be, quite secure. To any mere peasant ambling past this point on the headland's interior edge, there appeared nothing but bedrock overgrown with large ferns. However, behind the ferns would have been seen a *lip* of bedrock, and beneath it a snug, well-sheltered abode. Indeed, one fit for a king.

And so here it was his majesty's evening came to a close. Nestled inside, he soon closed his eyes and breathed deeply, drifting into sleep sufficiently content that within his island kingdom, all was well and good.

21

Thanksgiving on Whisper Island that year was even more than its usual festive affair. To begin, standing together on the island's headland on the sunny Saturday afternoon of that weekend, George and Marcy exchanged vows. As the groom so wished the ceremony itself was small and simple, with merely the islanders attending. But compensating for spare trimmings were myriad red and yellow autumn leaves that descended on the newly-wed couple when they ultimately embraced. The timing of the headland's gusting breeze, the hopeless romantics of the day all agreed, couldn't have been better.

Marriages were naturally give and take, though, and what Marcy gave away in "fanciness" on Saturday she steadfastly took back on Sunday. Thanksgiving supper doubled as wedding supper, and few supposed Marcy's cottage, at any point in its lengthy history, had ever been so elaborately decorated. Pam delivered her to the island on the Thursday prior to Thanksgiving, and over the following three days Whisper's 'gals' transformed Marcy's cottage into an "autumn glory palace." They also spared no effort on dinner preparations; on Sunday the islanders would sit down to nothing less than a royal banquet.

But all knew, of course, they were celebrating more than

a wedding or Thanksgiving, and fittingly, this third reason for cheer was duly noted.

George Clarke looked and felt pretty slick in the brand new three-piece suit he wore on both Saturday and Sunday. "Even paid *nine bucks* to get one of those stylists to do up the noggin," he boasted to Roger and Evan. So slick did he look, in fact, that once again — for the 27th straight year — Roger suggested George deliver the evening's toast.

After standing before a hushed crowd — and after straightening, on 'the wife's' cue, his crooked bow tie — George offered the following:

> *Couple of words here and there, I guess*
> *She sure was a doozy of a wiggle*
> *But now we can take'er easy*
> *And get a few essentials done around here*
> *This chunk of rock ain't much*
> *A guy kind of wonders at all the fuss*
> *But here the bunch of us are now*
> *Duded up, married up*
> *And about to stuff ourselves*
> *Resting in the knowledge that all*
> *Well, seems to have worked out.*

And with that — and not a word more — the islanders of Whisper together raised their glasses.

ABOUT THE AUTHOR

Born in Scarborough in 1964, Robert Rea moved to Muskoka at age five. Upon completing high school he attended the University of Waterloo, where he earned a Bachelor of Science (BSc) and a Bachelor of Environmental Studies (BES). Since graduating he has travelled extensively throughout the world, and has authored three works of fiction — *A View To The North*, *Sun Dreams*, and *The Earth, the Stars, and Whisper*. He lives with partner Marilyn Smart, who greatly assists him in the development and promotion of his books.

The author is pleased to receive comments regarding any of his current books, or to receive inquiries into upcoming publications. He may be contacted at either of the following addresses:

Regular mail: Robert Rea
              Box 921
              Bracebridge, Ontario
              Canada
              P1L 1V2

E-Mail: maplelnd@muskoka.com

A National Best-Seller!
Now Available in an
Enhanced Edition

A VIEW
TO THE NORTH

A NOVEL BY

ROBERT REA

Written with humour, compassion, and insight, *A View To The North* explores what may prove the most complex and debated topic of this new century — the human relationship with wild nature.

When Bruce and Valerie Farrow move their city-raised family from Toronto to the wilds of Muskoka, their ten-year-old son worries this dramatic lifestyle change will prove turbulent — and his worries are soon justified. Reflecting as an adult, Lewis Farrow recounts the triumphs and tragedies of his earliest years living on a tiny Muskoka lake, and how the surrounding woods and colourful lake residents profoundly influence his later life. With an informal, down-to-earth narrative that ranges from humorous to heart-wrenching, A VIEW TO THE NORTH explores the complexities of the human relationship with 'Mother Nature'.

Also Available!

SUN DREAMS

SHORT STORIES BY

ROBERT REA

From the author of the National Best-Selling

A VIEW TO THE NORTH

comes

SUN DREAMS

"Stories are to a land as facets are to a diamond ...
Each may reflect from a different angle, but all lend
sparkle to the same precious stone."

So the stage is set for **SUN DREAMS**, a rich assembly of stories
blending mystery, humour, romance, tragedy, and adventure.
A colourful cast offers not only a collective portrait of
Muskoka but insight into the many 'faces' all lands possess.
Written in the informal, down-to-earth style for which the
author has become known, **SUN DREAMS** explores the human
role in the nature of place.

"... as a group [the stories] provide a rich and varied tapestry of the
characters who populate the shorelines and backroads of cottage
country."
Sally Gower, *The Cottage Times*

"... an ensemble of characters sure to touch every reader lucky
enough to meet them. ... In these seven stories Rea demonstrates
his mastery of character development ... "
Louise Gleeson, *The Muskokan*

ADDITIONAL COPIES

Free shipping within 3 days anywhere in Canada!

To obtain signed or unsigned copies of any MapleLand Press book by mail, order directly from:

MapleLand Press
Box 1285
Bracebridge, Ontario
Canada P1L 1V4

A VIEW TO THE NORTH © 2000, 2002
A novel by Robert Rea
Can. $20.00 (includes GST), U.S. $14.95

SUN DREAMS © 2001
Short stories by Robert Rea
Can. $16.00 (includes GST), U.S. $11.95

THE EARTH, THE STARS, AND WHISPER © 2003
A novel by Robert Rea
Can. $18.00 (includes GST), U.S. $13.45

Free shipping on orders from within Canada.

Orders from outside Canada:
    For single-book orders, please add
    Can. $4.00 (U.S. $3.00) shipping and handling.
    For multiple-book orders, please add
    Can. $4.00 (U.S. $3.00) shipping and handling for
    first book plus Can. $0.75 (U.S. $0.50) per additional book.

    Please allow up to six weeks for delivery.

All orders payable by cheque or money order.

Copies signed by the author:
    Provide book recipient's name (or names) if desired.
    Please note signed copies are not returnable.